Blood in
Nottingham

Blood in Nottingham

BLOOD IN THE MIDLANDS

Ken Bisulca

Rev. date: 11/21/2017

To order additional copies of this book, contact:
Xlibris
1-888-795-4274
www.Xlibris.com
Orders@Xlibris.com
769534

Dedication

This book is dedicated to all the friends and family that have supported me through good times and rough on both sides of The Pond. I also feel an acknowledgement be given to the authors of gothic, mystery and erotic literature upon whose shoulders I have stood with this work.

Contents

The "I Hate The Preface" Preface

It's true, I do hate the preface, I never read it, and I feel it useless. However, in this case, especially for my American friends, I feel it necessary to provide some information before I begin. I would like to let you know what general life was like in the mid 18th century. The reason I chose this period to begin my series is that this was a time of transition in England, after the Reformation and before the Industrial Revolution. And just prior to the War of Insurrection (known to you as The American Revolution).

England was still predominantly rural, like the rest of the continent. But England's agricultural output was more than any other European country. World trade was rising, and England was benefitting from exporting more grain than it was importing. Productivity and real wages were inching upwards. People's lives were improving materially. They were getting more in return for their labour. People could buy manufactured items.

A new interest in variety and consumerism had developed. The idea that it was okay to find delight in buying things was taking hold, and Christian abstinence developed during The Reformation was in decline. The Puritanism of Cromwell's time (ending 80 years ago) was fading and so too was adherence to Biblical criticisms regarding the accumulation or lending of money, but some older, more conservative members of society, still clung to the old ways. English men and women had begun wearing lighter and brighter clothing instead of heavy wool and linen. Meanwhile wrist-watches were still inaccurate curiosities, and people kept time by the ringing of church bells or town cryers in smaller communities.

These were times of increased literacy as overall European Enlightenment had reached maturity. Personal correspondence and other forms of writing were on the rise. Literate people gathered in groups interested in science or literature and a variety of scholarly journals were published. Book production had increased, as had newspaper distribution.

Shifting religious beliefs and rising commerce was accompanied by a decline in demand for religious uniformity (a step away from the belief that those with views different from their own were evil). With Copernicus, Galileo and Newton, a new optimism about the benefits of learning had arisen in conflict with the old and common belief that the world was a mystery never to be fathomed by humanity. Many, including people who believed in science, continued to believe in god's interventions, but the belief that the world functioned solely by god's magic was in rapid decline, as was the belief that all humanity needed to get by was spontaneity and proper religious attitude.

People in Britain drank, as usual, gambled and fought duels. There were still moralists who preached on the need of women to resist men inflamed by carnal desires and pornographic literature as well as the need of women to remain virgins until marriage. On the other hand, prostitution was rampant. A German visitor to London complained of passing a "lewd female" every ten yards on a December evening along Fleet Street, including prostitutes as young as twelve.

The language in this novel is a local phonetic approach to authenticate the Nottingham dialect, which is proported to be one of the most difficult to imitate. To achieve the proper affect, I've attempted to duplicate the wordage as the characters would have spoken them, or would have sounded to an outsider.

There are also some local colloquial phrases to again make the language more authentically real. Greetings such as "Ayup" or from a female "Ayup, me ducks" are the same as "Hi ya" or Hi ya, my dear"; and in England, the greeting "You all right?" is preferred to the usual, "How are you?" in America. When people leave each other, "ta ta" becomes "Tarrah" to a Notty. Also, many times "regular folks" even today, use "f's" in place of "th's" so, "with" sounds like "wiff" and "both", like "bowff" and "three" becomes "free".

In writing this novel in this way, I am hoping to lend some local colour to how each character would actually be speaking.

Tarrah then, everyone. Enjoy!

Chapter 1

THE FLYING HORSE

It's mid July, 1742, Charlie Buttersworth enters The Flying Horse Inn for his usual evening drink. It's a busier pub than some of the others, located at The Poultry section of Nottingham. There are some regulars at the bar and chatting on benches around the walls of the pub. There are low gaming tables where draughts, chess, or backgammon are being played by other patrons. There are also several groups of brightly coloured ladies all around looking for someone to spend time with, who look up and smile at Charlie, who removes his tricorner hat, steps up to the bar and puts his right foot on the wooden rail beneath.

Charlie is a 24 year-old, tall man of 5 feet and 10 inches with an athletic build of 14 stone. His light brown hair takes lard to stay in place, but then it has the odour of the sheep it came from. Usually, Charlie just lets it be and it falls wherever it wants to, as he did today.

"Ayup, Mikey, you all right ?" he touches his moustache and strokes his Van Dyke style beard, brown flecked with red.

"Yeah, you?" said Mikey Whealan, the barman. He's slightly shorter than Charlie, and a good bit rounder. He obviously likes the steak and kidney pies that his wife, Jenna, the cook, makes. Or he makes her think he likes then. "Brown ale and a Whiskey, then, Charlie?"

"No worries, mate. Sounds good ta me, Mikey. Just got a few shillings more from Old Man McGrey. He got paid more for his barley and rye that he sold to the brewers' and bakers', so passed some on to us as well. Great bloke, that one."

"Ayup, me ducks, so ya have some more ta spend on me, then", said a girl dressed in a bright yellow off-shoulder top and purple skirt that showed a lot of cleavage as she puts her leg on the chair next to him. Not that Charlie was complaining, mind. "Wanna have a time, love?"

"Not yet, Evie, I'll have a drink first, yeah?" He has been with Evie many times before, never has he been disappointed, she has always been well worth the money spent.

"Ok, sweetheart, I'll just be over at the table with me girls. Don't let anyone else get ya, yeah?" And she heads off, long red hair swishing behind her. As she goes, she winks a twinkling green eye back to Charlie.

"Already, mate? That lot, they're always looking for someone to keep their fannies warm… and occupied! But that Evie, she's got a right proper scratch for it. Hahahaha. Not only that, but she's an Observant, as well, can sence a hit from a mile off, lad. Mind your purse with that one."

An Observant can only be described as a person that can use their sences to make conclusions about a particular situation. Sherlock Holmes is thought to be the most famous Observant.

"Hahaha, she does have some magical powers, then, eh, Mikey?" Charlie adds.

"Right you are. Any word from Iain away at tha wars?" Mikey asks.

"Nah, nothin' yet, but the paper says that now there's troops in Georgia fighting them from Spain. I'm not due ta report till October, so I've got three months ta make some coin before that. Figure that's where I'm headed. Hopefully that's where *he* is. Be good ta see him, it's been a while"

"Good on ya till then, mate. Same again?" Mikey asks as he sees both Charlie's glasses empty.

"Why not. Gotta get primed for the evening ahead." Charlie says and looks over at Evie, who's smiling back at him. "Jenna make anything special tonight?"

"Yeah, we got some lovely lamb in today, so she's gone and made a shepherd's pie. Truly brilliant."

"Sounds lovely. Tell her ta put one up for me, yeah?"

"Will do, lad" says Mikey and heads back to the kitchen to let Jenna know.

As he's gone, the door to the pub opens and into the bar walks a bloke that Charlie has drunk with before. Again, the girls look up and smile at him. He is so tall and skinny that his clothes are literally hanging off him. His spectacles are loose on his long nose and his black hair is as unkempt as Charlie's. Gavin Thomson works at The Castle as a specialist in mathematics.

He steps up next to Charlie and asks if he's seen Mikey.

"He's getting me something ta eat, mate. He'll be right back." Charlie tells him. "you ok?"

"Oh, fine and you?" Gavin answers.

"Ay-up, me duck. You all right?" says a blond haired girl dressed in a forest green crop top and royal blue skirt who saunters right up to Gavin and puts her face in his. Her bright blue eyes dance as she speaks. She's obviously been here a while as she slurs her words as she addresses him, and her breath smells like whiskey to Gavin.

"I'm fine young lady. And you?"

"Me? I'm always really, really good." She says, takes his hand and puts it up to her top-covered breast. "I'm Nancy, dear. Fancy a go?"

"I don't think so, my dear. Mayhaps later. I'll seek you out, you don't need to pursue me again." Says Gavin, removing his hand.

"Suit yourself." She shrugs, "I'll be here, darlin'." And leaves with a wink and a wry smile.

Mikey returns and moves to where Gavin is stood. "Charlie, be done in a tick. What'll it be then, Gavin?"

"May I kindly have a glass of brandy, Mikey?"

"No worries, Gav. How's tha maths business goin'?"

"Fine, thank you. We're debating Newton as opposed to Leibniz again. They're both brilliant, but I seemingly always have to play peacekeeper between the two camps." explained Gavin.

"What about you, Mikey, give us a go?" Nancy asks, looking him up and down. "Been a while since we had a tumble, eh? Fancy a free sample?" And she lifts her skirt exposing her fanny. She pats it with her other hand and a few drops of liquid seep down her leg.

"Keep it down, Nancy, you know how Jenna is. And no, not after you already been with half the bar." Charlie retorts.

"That's all right, then, made a fair crown tonight, anyways," and she taps her purse at her waist and she away to her table with some other girls.

"I can't sort it out, that maths." Says Charlie, "I can barely count the hooves on me horse. Hahahaha!"

"Very funny, indeed, Charlie." Says Gavin, smiling politely.

"That'll be one pound, 3 an' 6." Says Mikey as he delivers Charlie's meal: a large portion of shepherd's pie, mushy peas and a large chunk of crusty bread with an accompanying pot of butter."

"Cheers, mate. Krikey, prices *have* gone up, Mikey. May have ta start cookin' on me own." quips Charlie.

"Just as you're gettin' more, and McGrey's gettin' more, Porter's Bakery's gettin' more, so I gotta charge *you* more, yeah? It all goes round, doesn't it?"

"S'pose so, mate." And Charlie starts eating. "Fantastic!! Let Jenna know, I said so."

The door to The Flying Horse opens again, and in she walks. Well, not walking exactly, more like gliding. This woman is not one of your local girls; she is stately. Dressed all in deep blue, from the hat sitting atop her perfectly coiffed hair to the shoes on her delicate feet. Her dress is made of only of the finest materials with an identically coloured scarf clasped at her neck and deep blue gloves and a blue lacy veil finish off the entire kit. She moves over to the bar, next to Charlie, on the other side of Gavin, even though there are a fair few in the pub, he doesn't hear her footsteps as she moves.

"May I have a glass of claret," she asks Mikey, with an accent he doesn't recognise. She is definitely not from around here.

"Comin' up, m' lady." He responds and pours her a wine glass full.

"That'll be 3 shillings 4. Don't get much of call for claret around here, dear."

She hands him a one pound coin and responds: "*This* is the smallest I have, I am sorry."

Handing her back the change, Mikey asks: "So you on holiday, then?"

"I am... visiting." She purrs.

"What're you called, love?" he asks.

"I am Aleera." She answers.

"Never heard *that* name before. Where ya from then, dear?" Mikey asks again.

"I am from... across the water. I am looking for a quiet place to... live." She replies, getting agitated.

"Woulda thought you'd be better off in London." He comments.

"I have *been* to London, there were too many... questions." And Aleera shoots him a look that says, "Don't ask another."

"Right, I'll leave ya to it then." Mikey says. "I'm Mikey and if you need anything… right." Seeing her obvious annoyance, and he moves back to chat with some of the other regulars.

"You ready fer me now, dear?" It's Evie, back at Charlie's elbow as he's just finished his meal. Her intoxicating perfume disguising the slight odour of sex on her. "I've been waitin' for *you*."

"Not now, Evie. By the by, how many am I today, then?" Charlie says, eyes on Aleera the whole time.

"Only three, but I washed after the last one!!"

"Get off!!" Charlie says as he feels light fingers on his purse at his belt.

"Can't blame a girl fer tryin', can ya?" she says. "Fine, see if I give you a bargain again!"

"Tarrah, then." He calls as she stalks off. "Don't be so moody, Evie."

"Ya better watch out fer that one, Charlie. She ain't quite right, if you take my meanin'." She calls back.

"So, Aleera," Charlie says. "I'm Charlie. Fancy another claret? Oh, you haven't finished your first. Sorry."

"Thank you, Charlie. You are very charming." She says in her sultry accent. As she looks at him, he feels his blood start to rise in his face as she pulls up her veil.

Aleera's eyes are piercing and her smile is measured. Charlie thinks he sees just a hint of slightly larger canine teeth he hadn't noticed before. But her eyes keep him focussed above that.

"My carriage is just outside awaiting my return, Charlie. Would you care to join me?" She asks.

"Yeah!" Charlie says enthusiastically, guess it's gonna be a good night after all, he things. "Gotta say my tarrah's if you don't mind."

"Go on then." Mikey says. "We'll hold it down here for ya, mate." And gives Charlie a smiling wink.

Evie comes running over. "Do be careful, Charlie. As I said, something's not right there. You can stay and give *me* a go, yeah?"

"Cheers, love," he says and touches her on the cheek sweetly. "I'm always careful, you know me."

"Charlie, are you coming?" Allera calls from the open doorway.

"Right there, love." He grabs his hat and heads out the door.

Chapter 2

ALEERA'S HOME

Aleera's carriage is an ornate one, black with gold scroll-work, completely covered with dark curtains and deep blue carpetting on the floor. Once inside with the driver in position, Charlie's erotic nature takes hold. They ride along, kissing, fondling, and desperately seeking her flesh beneath the folds of her dress.

"Easy, Charlie," she says between kisses. "There's no time to rush. We have all night, my love."

"Sorry Aleera," he says, "I'm more used ta those girls at tha pub. I'm not sure how fast ta go with a classy bird like you." He was unquestionably sure, but as she said, he had all night.

The proceed to ride along past The Castle, on to North Street, then to the Mansfield Road, holding, kissing and groping each other all the way. Again, Charlie feels the blood rising in his face and groin. He is getting erotically heated, but Aleera, despite her own hands all over him and moaning delightedly, feels quite cool to the touch. On and on they ride in the carriage to the northwest of the city.

Finally, in what seemed like too short a time to Charlie, unless their destination holds even more pleasure, they slow. "Red Hill Cemetary" sign is directly ahead of them.

"Is that where we're headed, then love?" Charlie asks.

"You would be surprised how inexpensively you can purchase a home near places that you will have no noisy neighbours." She answers.

"Yeah, I bet". He says unsurely.

"We are here." She says, as they pass through the gate. She starts to straighten her dress before getting out of the carriage. The driver opens the door and pulls down the step to the carriage. Charlie gets out first, after tying up his trousers at the waist again, which Aleera had undone, feeling for his organ, swelled with pleasure. Once on the ground, Charlie helps Aleera down to the ground. Her dress, still not looking as neat as it had in The Flying Horse, and her hat and veil in her other hand. Again her hand is cold as ice.

"Come. Let us go inside." She says seductively. She pays the driver and they head inside.

"My pleasure, m'lady."

"Not yet, but it soon will be, my love." Aleera coos.

They hold hands as they enter her home. A fire is burning in the fireplace, but there are no signs of anyone living there other than that.

"Do you want another drink?" she asks Charlie.

"Got any whiskey?" he asks.

"Of course."

"Care ta join me? I hate to drink alone." He explains.

"No thank you, whiskey makes me choke." She tells him.

"Some more claret then." He suggests.

"I have had enough… for now." She says. "Bring it up to the bedroom. We will be more comfortable there."

Charlie pours himself a drink from the decanter, and joins Aleera on the stair. Arm-in-arm they head up to the bedroom, kissing and re-kindling the passion begun in the carriage. Most of his drink spills on the staircase.

"Do not concern yourself, my servants will take care of that." She comforts him as she sees Charlie looking down. "I will have more sent up if you desire at some point."

They mutually open the door to the expansive bedroom.

"You may get undressed, my love," she says and Aleera excuses herself to the walk-in wardrobe. Charlie quickly disrobes and gets himself under the sheets and duvee on the high bed. His organ is throbbing as he takes a large gulp finishing his whiskey, and he strokes himself in anticipation.

Aleera emerges through the door to the wardrobe wearing a sheer chest-to-floor length white robe, open in the middle and a white ribbon around her neck. She moves smoothly across the room, lust in her eyes, and… "Are those canine teeth slightly larger again?" Charlie thinks, then puts it out of his mind as she joins him on the bed.

He grabs her breasts beneath the robe, sucks at her nipples. He unties the ribbon on her neck, notices two small puncture wounds and kisses where the ribbon had been. Aleera moans in delight and grasps his organ, pulling and tugging on it, licking the juice emerging from the tip. She rips the robe off and throws it onto the floor as she is now completely nude. Charlie rolls Aleera on her back and inserts his hand inside of her body. Wet, oh yes, but also still as cold as could be.

"Ain't you gettin' excited?" he asks.

"My dear, I have seldom felt so much passion, I knew you were the one I was looking for when I watched you over the last three weeks." She tells him.

She kisses him and rolls him over so that she is on top now His organ sticking straight up engorged with erotic energy. She takes it in her hands and inserts him inside her as she throws her head back, her blond hair cascading down her back and her nipples are erect as erotic passion overtakes her. They roll over and over, moaning, crying out, and cumming again and again, and finally separating to catch their respective breaths.

"My dear boy, you certainly have stamina, I will say that." She says breathlessly.

"Is that a good thing?" he asks.

"Oh sweetheart, it's the best thing. I knew you would be wonderful." Aleera says dreamily. "Now that we have given your pleasure satisfaction, it is time for mine."

"I don't know what ya mean." Charlie says.

"Let me show you." And she rolls over on top of him again and pins his arms down with her knees. She sucks and kisses his neck and then Charlie feels the sting of her teeth. Something warm seeping out… is that my blood?

"Oi! What ya on about? Stop. Stop!!" he implores her, but she doesn't stop.

She continues draining his body of his vital fluid. Charlie tries to get her off of him, but she is surprisingly strong. She still pins his arms down on the bed and he feels himself getting weaker all the time as she seems to get stronger by the second.

"It is your turn now, my love." She informs him. "Your turn to drink."

She places her fingers between her heaving breasts and with her index finger nail, creates an incision in her flesh. The blood oozes out of the cut and she takes hold of Charlie's head and places his lips on the slice.

"Drink. Drink!" she implores him. "It will make everything much better, you will see."

Against his normal judgement he drinks the warm liquid issuing from the cut in her chest. Again Aleera moans in pleasure, and he's sure he feels her orgasm on his fingers, which, in his semi-conscious state, he finds somehow are inside of her again. She pulls his head away from her breasts and attends to his neck again. Charlie loses consciousness, then his entire body goes limp.

Chapter 3

A NEW MAN

Charlie awakens on his own bed in his cottage. He feels odd as he rises. He wonders if what happened with Aleera had actually happened or not. How long has he been asleep? The sun is shining, so it must be the next morning.

He separates the curtains on the window to see the day ahead. At once, Charlie feels his skin burning hot from the rays of the yellow orb in the sky. He draws the curtain again, as his skin starts to cool and return to normal.

"Get over." He says. "What the fuck has that twat done ta me?"

Suddenly there's a knock at Charlie's door.

"Charlie, you in? It's Evie. Ain't seen you since Wednesday when you left with that cow. You all right, love? We was all worried.

"What day is it today? How long have I been asleep?" He thinks as he reaches up and touches his neck, finding two tiny vertical puncture wounds slightly below his left ear. He feels the same two puncture wounds that he saw on Aleera's neck at her house. "Can't come out right now, love" Charlie calls to Evie through the door. "I'll see ya at The Horse tonight, sweetheart."

"You sure, love?" she calls back. "We was all wondering since ain't seen ya. Tell ya what, I won't have no other bloke before *you* tonight. How's that?"

"Sounds like you'll be more than ready by then, dear," Charlie replies. "Say, what day is it, then, love? I've lost track of time."

"Oh, don't you worry, lad, I'll have a good scratch on fer ya by tha time I see *you*." Evie answers slyly. "It's Friday all day, by tha way, the night fer gettin' randy! Can't wait, love!" She informs him. "Tarrah, then, sweetheart," she knocks a pattern of good-bye and he hears her sachet off.

Friday! How can it be Friday? What the fuck!! And Evie, as Mikey said when last he was at the Flying Horse, is always on the pull. Her pussy must get tingly since she hasn't shagged each and every hour!!!

All of a sudden Charlie finds himself aroused at the thought of getting with Evie again, but now, it's not only his groin that is growing, but his canine teeth start to protrude slightly. He touches one of them: "Ow!" he says and notices that his finger is bleeding from the puncture, but it stopped instantly. It didn't seem that a small increase in size could cause such a deep wound. But now, at the sight of his blood, the canines seem to grow a bit larger.

"What *is* happening?" He says out loud. "That Aleera slag must have done something ta me. I gotta find her and sort it out."

He puts on his hat to go out, opens the front door and it's like his entire body is on fire… Charlie slams the door again and at once his skin is restored to its normal form.

"Well, THAT won't work." He says. "Guess I'll wait till tonight and see her then."

He then sits and wonders to himself about his job at the mill. He's sure that Old Man McGrey has missed him; he's the best grain packer there. He looks at the clock, which reads twenty-five to seven, it would be another four hours before the sun goes down. So, being famished, Charlie decides to make something to eat. There iss leftover cooked beef and some potatoes in the root cellar. So he puts a kettle on and lights the stove. He puts the beef and two potatoes in the oven and when the kettle starts to whistle, puts some tea in a bit of cheese cloth, closes the top with a piece of twine and puts it and the hot water in a mug. After giving it about five minutes to steep, he adds his sugar and milk.

He has no sooner put the mug to his lips than he feels violently sick!! He smells the milk and it smells fine. He had only got it yesterday… oops, well Monday, that would be. He takes another sip and, sure enough, again he feels off-colour and starts to vomit.

"What is goin' on *here*, then," Charlie wonders as his food continues to cook.

Once he thinks it's done, he puts the beef and potato on a plate along with a mug of brown ale he brought home from the Flying Horse a few days ago.

"Maybe tha tea was bad… but the ale, never!" Charlie surmises.

He takes a bite of the beef, and even though it's re-heated completely, he gags and spits it out. The same response occurs for the potato… and the ale just makes him actually spew!

Just as he was ready to give it up, across the floor, from where it came Charlie knew not, scampers a mouse. It stops just short of the wall across the way and Charlie's blood starts rising in his face again. Instantly, his blood rises in his neck and he feels very hot. The canine teeth in his mouth start growing and his vision sees everything as red-tinged. The mouse starts moving toward the wall again.

"Wait" he calls to it as if that would do anything, but surprisingly, the mouse has stopped dead in its tracks.

Charlie leaps off his chair in a flash and onto the mouse, gashing its body and drinking the mouse's blood till it is dry. All of a sudden he feels a little better, as he has finally had something to eat after five days. Although he feels better, and still ravenously hungry, but mentally he is undergoing quite a conundrum. But at least his teeth are back to normal and his vision has cleared.

"That continental bitch," Charlie swore. "She's turned me into a bloody monster!!"

Charlie is finally realising what changes he has undergone in the time he was asleep. He had been changed into the same creature of the night that Aleera was already. He feels his neck again and there are the same two little puncture wounds still vertically situated just below his right ear.

Charlie decides to change clothes for the night ahead and finds a claret shirt and scarf, which he ties around his neck, and medium brown trousers, claret stockings, brown boots and his favourite tricorner hat. Then looks into the mirror to find… nothing. Nothing at all. He sees the shirt, scarf and hat, but they are hanging and sitting on nothing. There is no image of Charlie in the mirror. This only confirmed his original hypothesis that he is indeed a vampyre.

What is he to do now? Fortunately, as he looks at the clock, he sees that it is ten to eleven and the sun has sunk already. He opens the front door and nothing happens, so he steps out into the night air.

His horse, Chauncy, is still in the stable from the last evening he rode home from his job, before he went to The Flying Horse and left with Aleera. Chauncy is a tall horse, maybe eighteen hands high, but quick and sturdy as well. He is chestnut coloured with golden main and tail, with a very pleasant disposition. Charlie saddles, bridles, and mounts him, and at first the horse is unsure what to do. It's only after he hears Charlie's voice say, "Get up, boy" that he starts walking out of the stable. He rides out onto Stoney Street, turning to the northeast, along the Mansfield Road, following the route he had taken with Aleera in her carriage.

When he gets to the Red Hill Cemetary, he rides on through the gate and up to the house at the end of the lane, slinging his rucksack bag over his shoulder.

There is only one problem, as he knocks at the door, there is no answer, so he pushes the door and to his surprise, it is open and he walks inside. The fire has gone out, and there is even less furniture in the downstairs area than when he had been there before. Walking upstairs, there is no bed, no clothes and no furniture in either the room or in the wardrobe. It seems that Aleera has returned to her continental home. She is the only one, he thought, that could steer him on his new path. What is he to do now? Well, there is always Evie waiting for him at the Flying Horse. Maybe she could take his mind off of his recent dilemma.

He leaves the house in Red Hill and rides southeast toward the centre of the city. Upon arriving at the Flying Horse, he sees Evie, standing seductively outside next to the door, her bare left foot up against the wall drinking her whiskey and water.

"I've been waitin' for ya, lover." She tells him as he walks up. She's dressed in a midnight blue dress, cut up to her hip and wide shoulder cut-outs. Clearly she is wearing nothing beneath her kit.

Charlie could feel his blood rising in his face and groin, one more time. He could also feel his canine teeth start to lengthen.

"What ya on about?" she asked him. "Thought you might like this colour, after all, that cunt you were with on Tuesday wore it then. What ya think?" and she twirled round, showing off obvious assets. "Like?"

"Oh, yeah, I do like it, love." He could feel the blood, what little there was remaining from his snack of the mouse, begin to really boil now. He could also feel his canine teeth lengthen further until he could no longer close his mouth for their protrusion and he put his hand over his mouth pretending to stroke his mustache. His eyes burnt red and the vein in her neck was outlined as if there was a light within it.

As he neared Evie, she commented, "So, undergone some changes I see. Reddy eyes, long teeth, almost clear skin... You should know that my gran'mum was a gypsy, and she told me about your lot. Seein' all rosey, yeah? Can't get on a day without blood, so she said. And if this is your first day out, she told me that you take on the like of those that ya feed on."

Charlie's head was spinning with this news, but obviously Evie knew much more about his condition than he did. So, maybe he didn't need to hunt for Aleera after all. But as he thinks and calms down, his teeth are again back slowly receding back to normal. Not completely, mind, but somewhat.

"I'll have ta see ya later, Evie, gonna go in and have a pint or two, then I'll be back, yeah?"

"Won't do ya no good, my fine fella." She says, cheerily, staring at her finger nails, swinging her hips, balancing on her bare foot still against the wall. "You'll see, but I'll be waitin' here when ya come back on out, darlin'."

Charlie walks inside and sees Gavin at the bar. Mikey must be in the back ordering or getting food.

"Ayup, Gav", he says to Gavin as he silently moves next to him.

"Oh, Charlie, I didn't hear you approach, my good fellow." Gavin replies.

"Fancy a bit of fresh air, mate? It's kinda nasty in here." Charlie says.

"Yes, I'll take my drink with me, if you don't mind." Gavin informs him.

They move outside together, Gavin chatting about something mathematical as they pass Evie next to the door. All the while, Charlie's entire being is focussed on the unfortunate task at hand. His canines lengthen again, and his vision is red-filled. He can hear Gavin's heartbeat loudly in his ears and sees the vein in his skinny neck as if it were a thin river of blood. His hunger is overcoming Charlie and the urge is overwhelming.

They round the corner of the pub into the alley beside. As soon as they're both out of sight, Charlie strikes. He covers Gavin's mouth with his strong hand, Gavin's glass tossed to the ground, Charlie bends Gavin's head, so that the carotid artery is exposed, and with the blood pounding in his ears, head and temples, he sinks his large canine teeth into Gavin's neck and drinks deeply. Gavin tries to scream, but Charlie's hands are still covering his mouth, He scratches, tugs, and beats Charlie with his fists, but the vampyre is undeterred. He drains his body of the precious red liquid and poor Gavin slumps to the floor of the alley.

Charlie, however, feels MUCH better, different than he did before, after all he hadn't had anything to eat... or drink... since Tuesday. His vision is amazingly clear, his teeth, which he feels for, are completely back to normal and he wipes the drops of blood away from his mouth with Gavin's left sleeve.

Gavin's body lays to the ground, devoid of any life, eyes wide open in horror, knowing he was about to die. "I have to get rid of the body," Charlie thinks. He HATES what he has to do, but what would he say if they found Gavin's decomposing flesh intact in the alley? How could he possibly explain the events of his uncontrollable hunger? How could he tell Iain of the irresistible urge that overtook him? Of the ache in his entire body until he fed on poor Gavin? What could he say if they asked him how and why that unlucky lad was sucked dry? He might be put to death if he is caught. Or maybe he'd get lucky and just get sent to the American colonies. "Well, fitting as I just took Gavin's life, I suppose." He thinks.

So he starts on his task. Devoid of blood, the body is surprisingly light as Charlie lifts his former mate to his shoulder. Around the back of the pub is the rubbish pile. Clearly it hasn't been taken away in a while. It smells putrid and there is food, broken plates and glasses, and rotting grains from the barrels of ale in the cellar. Charlie quickly disrobes Gavin and breaks off his arms and legs, secreting them in the middle of the pile. He takes the remaining torso, rips it in half, and tossing the ribs on top of the pile and shoving the rest under the entire mess. Finally, he takes Gavin's clothes and wipes his hands and dusts his clothes, placing the dirty clothes in his satchel.

Charlie rounds the corner again to find Evie still stood against the wall, brushing her hair aimlessly, glass of red wine in her hand, one bare foot still against the wall.

"Told ya, love." She says carelessly as he passes. "Feelin' any better now, love?"

Charlie stops and looks at her.

"What do you mean, my dear?" He says. He recognised his own voice, but the words were not familiar to him. He had never spoken quite so well.

"Well, look at ya: all a proper gent now. Wiped most of tha blood off ya, anyway. Was he good for ya? You ain't still hungry, are ya?" She asks.

"No, I'm not still hungry." He responds.

"Well, now ya been sated, still fancy a toss?" she asks

"Clearly, that would be lovely, Evie. We can go on back to mine, then, yeah?" He was anxious to learn more of her assessment of his situation. He holds his arm out, she takes it and they head off down the High Pavement Street toward his cottage.

Evie's Observant skills come into fore as they walk, as she skillfully avoids the sharp stones, shards of broken glass and numerous varieties of manure on the roads to his house. Charlie, too notices and avoids the same hazards, even though she does it more nonchalantly and he has shoes on *his* feet. He can see the hazards clearly as the moon is full that night.

"Ya know what they say about a full moon, don't ya?" Evie asks dreamily as they walk.

"Not sure what you mean, there are a lot of things." Charlie replies, looking briefly up.

"Well," she says, "me gran'mum says that with those whispy clouds passing by the full moon, they calls it a 'Howlin' Moon', 'cause that's when tha werewolves come out."

"Ah, yes. I have heard that one." He says. "Never believed in werewolves before, but then I never exactly believed in vampyre's either. So, I guess…"

The conversation ends as they arrive at Charlie's cottage and he holds the door open for her to enter.

"Why thank you, my good sir." Evie acknowledges.

Once inside, they separate, and Charlie lights some candles in the front room. He turns back to Evie, who undoes one clasp at the waist of the dress and it falls to the floor. Her hair falling over her shoulders, providing the only covering to her exposed body down to her navel.

"Saves time in a hurry." She explains, smiling.

Indeed she has nothing underneath. She spreads her feet and puts her hands on her hips. Charlie feels that rise of blood in his groin and his neck. His vision is turning red, as he looks at Evie's naked body. It is *truly* spectacular, with her long red hair just over her shoulder, green eyes bright and twinkling through her fringe, her breasts, ample and nipples erect, and with her legs apart, she is now touching herself through her red pubic hair. The vein on her neck appearing to Charlie as highlighted, despite the dim light of the room... His canines are already elongated, the blood now pounding in his ears.

"Two crowns, Charlie, you know the rules. I get paid first." She tells him.

"Of course, Evie, let me just get it." And Charlie turns and acts like he's about to get the amount she demands, but before taking a single step, quick as a wink, he is upon her, sinking his elongated canine teeth into her gorgeous neck and drinking thirstily. She tries to fight him off at first, sinking her nails deep into his back and pounding on it. But then her strength starts waning, and she sinks into his arms. He doesn't finish her off, but releases his hold as he feels her weaken.

"Now it's *your* turn, Evie. Drink before I do you in." he instructs her. He then opens his tunic at the chest, and with his index finger, cuts a long incision in his chest as he had seen Allera do when he was "turned". He grasps her head, and, remembering what was done to him clearly, holds her face up to the gaping wound. "This way we can be together here in Nottingham."

"I can't Charlie, don't make me." She says dreamily, but in her weakened state, she is no match for his strength. He holds her tightly against his chest and she has no alternative but to drink as he directed her. He feels ecstatic as she drinks and leans his head back as he orgasms for the first time, hopefully, that night.

After a bit, he pulls her away from him, her mouth covered with his blood, and continues drinking from her naked body. If he was made into a vampyre this way, maybe SHE could be as well. "It'd be nice to have a companion like Evie," he reasons.

After he is done, Charlie carriees her limp body to his bed. He has no idea where she lives, if she even has a permanent address. Additionally, he now becomes aware of many things around him. He looks over at the dish he was trying to eat dinner on and sees it has a chip in the rim. How did he not see that small hole at the base of the east wall? That must be how the mouse got in. My favourite painting on the wall is also not straight, which is important as that's where I keep any extra moneys from Old Man McGrey. How did he not notice these things before? Evie definitely would have done... ah yes, what did she say about the First Day out? Taking on the traits of those upon whom he fed? Guess that actually was true.

Chapter 4

GETTING A SUPPLY

As Evie "slept" naked beneath the sheets and duvet his bed, although she wasn't breathing, Charlie calculated that he couldn't continue taking lives to satisfy his hunger. He would either be caught and killed, or, if not, he would run out of his blood supply eventually. The slags in the pubs wouldn't be missed (more money for the survivors, he deduced), but others with families, responsibilities, and brethrens. No, he couldn't put himself through the mixed emotions of disgust, repulsion and exhilaration that he felt with Gavin. Suddenly his powers of deduction seem much acuter than they ever had before.

As Charlie walks back to the Flying Horse, he is thinking all along the way. He decides to talk with Mikey and see if he has any suggestions as to his present situation. Mikey has to deal with a lot as a barman. He might have heard or known more about or, like Evie, been told stories by an elder that might have been through something similar in ages past.

Charlie arrives at The Flying Horse sooner than he usually took. He opens the door and sidled in and up to the bar.

"Ay-up, Mikey. You ok?" Charlie says brightly.

"Yeah, fine, mate. So, finally decide ta show your mush around here, eh?" Mikey says, teasingly. "Gavin was here a while ago, lookin' for ya. Ya seen him, then?"

"No, I haven't seen him tonight." Charlie lied. Again, his terminology is entirely different from the way he normally spoke.

"Well, my boy, you sure sound different. Been studyin' up at the Castle with Gavin, then? Mightn't he want to inspect your homework?" and he chuckles. "Maybe that's why her was here! Hahahaha."

"Yes, I'm sure that's it, Mikey." Charlie replied hesitatingly. "I noticed the odour coming from the rubbish in the back. They coming to get it soon? You could be losing folk who want to come in for a pie and pint, mate."

"Yeah, Farmer Williams is coming tomorrow mornin' with a large cart to put it on his compost as usual. I know how bad is smells out there." Mikey says. "And you could be right. Jenna told me tha same."

"That's good, Mikey, it'll be a relief, I'm sure. Say, there's another matter I need to speak with you about if you don't mind."

"No worries, mate. How can I help?" the barman asks

"It's really a dodgy matter that needs privacy." Charlie tells him.

"Fine. I'll get Jenna up front here. And we on go in back." And he leaves.

"Fancy a twirl, Charlie?" It's Nancy, her sheer white puffy shirt showing off her ample breasts and flowey print skirt that she keeps touching at her crotch. In between, she brushes her long blonde hair. Maybe she has a disease from all the sex she's had. Charlie observes barely-noticeable dirt stains on her skirt at the knee and identifies her patchouli perfume, again disguising the sex she's obviously had.

"Not tonight, Nancy. Many thanks."

"You on with Evie again? Ain't seen *her* in a bit, lad." Nancy says sarcastically.

Mikey returns with his wife in tow. She's a short, pleasant-looking woman, dark hair, pulled tight around the back, thick through the waist, wearing a print dress and apron both of which are dotted with flour, blood and bits of gravy.

"Go on ya slag!" Jenna says. "No one wants YOUR dirty cunt!"

"And no one wants your nasty cake hole." Nancy retorts drunkenly.

"Right, out ya go fer *that* one." Jenna says and moves quickly from behind the bar, surprisingly for large woman, grabs her blond hair and back of her waist, and shoves her out the door. "And don't come back, twatbag!!"

"Well," she says Charlie and Mikey as she returns. "Now that *that* rubbish is out, you lot go on then with yer *men talk*. I'll handle things out here." and steps back behind the bar.

"Thank you, Jenna," Charlie says and the men walk to the kitchen where Mikey turns to face Charlie.

"So, what's on your mind, then, Charlie?" Mikey asks.

And Charlie tells him about the encounter with Aleera almost the week prior and the consequences of his prurient actions.

"A vampyre? Are you sure." Mikey says. "Now I ain't positive, but heard of them being on the continent, but never around here. Someone called Dracula, as I recollect. Killed a lot of people, from what I heard from me cousin in tha wars. He's seen and heard a lot o' stories."

"Look, Mikey, I don't wanna kill anyone." Charlie says.

"Well that's good news." Mikey says, relieved. "From what I know about these things, and mind, it ain't much, ya need some blood every day. 'Course ya could start killin' folks, but that ain't really a good idea, yeah? And you already said that ya don't wanna do that anyway."

"Are you sure I need blood every day ta survive, mate?" Charlie asks, noticing that as his hunger grows, he reverts back to his usual way of speaking. "I'd really hate to hafta start doin' folks in just so I can carry on."

"That's what me cousin says." Mikey says. "Now, we might wanna see if *any* type of blood will do ya. That would solve a lot of problems for all of us. And you too, mate. Look, there's a fresh-killed cow hanging in back we just got in from Boyle's Butcher's with a bowl underneath to catch the blood. Give it a go, lad."

Mikey leads Charlie out in the back. Sure enough, hanging there is the newly-dead cow with his tongue hanging loosely from his mouth. Charlie immediately spots the large ceramic pot of fresh blood underneath; there's even blood still dripping from the carcass' mouth. Charlie's vision goes red again, and his canine's enlarge. Quicker than Mikey could see, Charlie is eagerly lifting the bowl, drinking the warm liquid inside eagerly. It is completely gone in a few seconds. Charlie's vision returns to normal and his teeth recede to their normal length.

"Many thanks for your assistance, Mikey. You have truly given me great assistance." He tells the barman. "This has saved a great many, including me, a great deal of suffering, whilst allowing me to maintain my existence," noticing for the first time since he has been coming to The Flying Horse, a scar above Mikey's eyebrow and under his nails, is dirt of the same type as from outside the pub, just like the one on Nancy's dress.

"Well, mate." Mikey replies. "Looks like I gotta get in a bunch of cow's blood for ya. In tha winter-time, it's no issues keepin' a large supply fresh, but now in tha summer, gonna hafta come in and get it daily. Now good job that Boyle don't keep it, but for about a pint, when he makes his blood pudding. He throws tha rest away, he does. I'm hoping if I ask nice-like he'll give me tha rest for free! And wouldn't *that* be nice, eh?"

"That would be glorious, Mikey. Cheers very much, mate. See you tomorrow then, you're about to shut anyway."

"Yeah, you're right." Says Mikey. "Jenna and me got a date night... can't wait!!"

As Charlie leaves the Flying Horse, and starts walking home, he comes upon Nancy stood under a lamppost that's flickering in the still night. Since he has fed, his powers of observation, even in this dim light, are highly accentuated. He notices several stains on her blouse and dress instead of the just the one he saw in the Horse. The one on her collar appears to be blood or maybe raspberry jam or lip colouring. Could be any of those at this point, he thinks. Another stain at her middle just above the cut of the blouse appeared to be gravy in the shape of lips. There's a third one in the middle of her skirt, slightly above the soil one, a white one, that she keeps touching and putting up to her nose. Further there are red hand prints on each side of Nancy's neck. She's been a busy girl all right.

"Oi, Charlie, what a cow that Jenna is, eh?" she says, still feeling the effects of drinking most of the day. "Fancy a tumble? I got some time, now."

"Many thanks Nancy, again, but I've got to get back home." Charlie says, even though he *very* much would like to shag Nancy... or anyone. But he had only been with her once, and it was not exactly memorable, but at the time, it was "any port in a storm", as the saying goes.

As he leaves her behind, Charlie hears Nancy propositioning another possible patron. Walking further on up the road, he passes Watchman William Masterson walking in the opposite direction. He's one of the paid police officers in Nottingham. Tall, sturdy, brown hair and eyes, and a burly moustache, he's dressed in his cotton navy blue tunic, trousers, and floppy hat identifying him as a Watchman.

"Ayup, Charlie," said Watchman Masterson. "Comin' from Tha Horse, eh?

"Yes," said Charlie, "figured I'd make an early night of it."

"Anything good happenin' or just another night?" the watchman asks absentmindedly as they shake hands. "Say, you must have caught cold from someone. Your hand's are freezin'!"

"Nothing really," Charlie replies, "only Nancy by the light on Fink Hill Street. And yes, that's why I'm heading home. I don't want to be sick working for Old Man McGrey. You know how he is."

"I do indeed," the watchman says. "Thanks, mate. I'll put her on her way before she gets into even more trouble. Heard about her and Jenna over at Tha Horse earlier."

"It was over very quickly. You know Jenna, Will." Says Charlie. "Well, cheers, mate." and he departs the conversation with another handshake.

"Cheers, Charlie," says the constable. "Hope ya feels better, lad."

It's a little over a mile walk back to his cottage. And he's halfway home when he hears the sound of a Watchman's whistle, meaning trouble of some type. He keeps on his path toward home, unconcerned. He's got enough on his mind anyway.

Chapter 5

AN ADJUSTMENT IN HIS LIFE

Uneventfully walking the rest of the way home, Charlie opens his front door and enters his cottage. He goes through the front room to the bedroom where the still naked Evie is silently recovering from her ordeal. By the same time-line he went through, it should be several more days before she regains herself, at which time, she'll need to feed. It'll be his responsibility to make sure she does so without harming anyone else.

The sun is just about to rise as he looks to the windows to assure the curtains are drawn, then undresses and gets into bed next to Evie. Her body is cold and skin translucent white, but the two puncture wounds on the right side of her neck are clearly visible, though not leaking blood. Charlie rolls onto his back and suddenly wonders what he'll do for money, after all, he will owe his landlord, Mrs. Powers his monthly rent of twenty-five pounds in two weeks. He'd better come up with something soon. Obviously, he'd have to let Old Man McGrey know that he could no longer work for him. So that opportunity is no longer an option.

Then he remembers that Gavin's clothes are still in his rucksack in the front room. Maybe... he rises and silently moves to the rucksack slung over the chair. Certainly there must be some coins in the pockets. Searching, there's nothing in the left one, but in the right, there are two whole sovereigns, four shillings and six farthings. Charlie is sure professors don't get paid all that much from The Castle, but surely there must be more than this. However, now that the sun has risen on this semi-overcast day, he would need to rest until tonight. He returns to his bed next to Evie, lays down on his back, folds his hands over his chest, closes his eyes and instantly is asleep… well, maybe not exactly asleep, more like dead, because he doesn't move, doesn't breathe, doesn't snore.

Charlie awakens to the sound of the neighbour's dog barking and barking and barking. He emerges from under the sheets and rises silently. Evie is still not awake/alive. The sun has set and it's raining outside, so it must be after ten at night. Charlie heads into his toilet for some soap and a towel. He hasn't cleaned up in several days and he can smell himself, so he's sure that others must be able to smell him as well. He steps outside into the rain, leaving the towel in a hook just inside the back door, and washes up in the alcove outside the back door. He feels better in one regard, but is now ravenously hungry. Once back inside, he grabs the towel and dries himself, then pulls on a yellow shirt, grey trousers and waistcoat, and white stockings with black boots from his wardrobe. He has to go see two people this evening after going to The Flying Horse: Mrs. Powers and Old Man McGrey.

Charlie pulls on his navy blue coat and goes out into the rain to the stable down the way, where Chauncy is being kept.

"Ayup, mate," cries Mr. Firthe, as Charlie takes down his saddle and begins to place it on Chauncy.

"Yeah, you?" Charlie answers.

"Off to Tha Horse and them trollops, then?" says the stable owner.

"Oi, everybody got ta make a livin', mate." Charlie says. He is famished, and had better get to the pub, as he can feel his vision start to grow red. He wouldn't want to have to feed on the man who keeps his horse in such good condition.

"Well, there's one less of 'em, now." Mr Firthe informed him. "One got herself killed last night. Been all over town, it has. You ok? You're lookin' a bit peaky, mate. Feelin' all right?"

"Yeah, I'm ok". Charlie says, covering his face with his hat. "Gotta head off then mate. Cheers."

"Tarrah, then, Charlie." Mr. Firthe calls as Charlie rides off. "Oh, and I'll need the stable fee when ya can get it."

Charlie rides quickly the little over a mile distance to The Flying Horse. His vision is getting redder and redder and his canines grow larger as he goes, so that by the time he gets to the pub, Chalrlie's hunger is almost unbearable again. But he also wonders about who got killed last evening. Nottingham is a small town and he can't remember a time when someone died of anything other that old age. He recalls the Watchman's whistle he heard on his way home last night... he might have just missed it!

Arriving at the pub, Charlie quickly ties up Chauncy outside and hurries inside. It's as busy as usual, with the normal crowd at the bar and benches, and the regular assortment of tarts in scattered groups... except for Evie and Nancy, of course, all chatting in low voices.

"Mikey!!" Charlie calls so loudly that all conversation around the bar stops. "Well, go on then! About your business!" he growls to the crowd, who return to their chatting as the barman appears form the back.

"Come on back, Charlie, come on back!" Mikey says. And Charlie follows him through the burlap drape behind the bar into the kitchen. "I got fresh sheep's blood today, mate. Let's see if this can make you feel better."

He brings a covered ceramic pot out from a cupboard underneath the sink. Charlie can barely see from the crimson in his sight and his canine teeth are so large that he can't close his mouth properly. Mikey removes the cover and hands the pot to Charlie. He grabs it and eagerly drinks, so desperate, that some of the precious liquid spills from around the corners of his mouth and down his chin and onto his shirt. He takes a second to breathe and wipes the blood travelling from his mouth with his finger and inserts it back to his awaiting mouth. Can't waste a drop, he thinks. He then lifts the pot again to his mouth and finishes off the rest of its contents.

"That feels ever so much better, Mikey. Cheers." He tells the barman. "This entire town and I owe you a great debt, mate."

"Well, you better clean up before ya go out there." Mikey tells him, handing him a soapy dish rag. Charlie takes it and dabs the few drops of blood from his yellow shirt as best he can.

"That's better, mate, c'mon, let's go." Together Mikey and Charlie walk from the kitchen back to the front of the pub, where the low din is still going on.

"No worries, Charlie," Mikey answers. "So sorry ya gotta go through this. I just wanna help."

"Cheers for that, mate. Listen, I've got some errands to run," Charlie tells him. "Be back later, lad."

"Tarrah, then, mate." And shakes Charlie's hand before he departs.

Charlie heads out before any of the many prostitutes can proposition him. He mounts Chauncy and heads off to see Old Man McGrey's farm first. It's a two-mile ride to the farm and it's late now. Charlie hears the Town Cryer sounding off "Eleven o' tha clock and all is well." He's sure that the farmer will be asleep, but with sunset at quarter past ten, he really doesn't have much of a choice. He kicks Chauncy gently in the sides, instructing him to gallop on.

It's only fifteen minutes before he arrives at Old Man McGrey's farm, he rides up the walkway to the front door and knocks, no response. He knocks again, no response again. Three times lucky, Charlie guesses, he knocks again and this time, Charlie sees a candle light flickering, hears Old Man McGrey walking toward the door.

"Who tha fuck!?" He hears McGrey swear.

"It's me, Charlie." He says.

Opening the door, Mr. McGrey says. "Charlie, where ya been, lad, we missed ya this week. Them other two lads together can't do what you can. Say, why you here so late. You know we gotta get up early in the morning. We got tha West Field ta harvest tomorrow." 'Old Man' McGrey is indeed an older man, slim and short with a long, full beard, mostly white with some grey bits as well. He stands inside the doorway in a white dressing gown and cap with long grey hair protruding beneath. It was unusual to see his hair without a ribbon for his pony-tail. A candle in its holder is clasped in his strong hands.

"This is why I'm here, Mr. McGrey," Charlie explained. "I have to let you know that I won't be able to work for you anymore. My situation has changed. However, I would like to perform some other duties for you, if I could. You have always been good to my dad and now me, so I want to do something for you. What I'm suggesting is that I compose a ledger for your farm. This way I'll be able to pay you back for all the kindness that you've shown to me and my family."

"Well," says McGrey. "That's interesting. I gotta think about that. Ya come here so late, tell me that ya can' work bagging no more, but now that ya got some learning, probably up Tha Castle, ya wanna do maths fer me. I *need* ya baggin' up grain, lad. I can manage tha ledger, m'self."

"Mr. McGrey, let me explain", insists Charlie, "and as I've said, my situation has changed, I can't work during the daylight hours, that's why I came over now."

"Explain, nothin'." McGrey replies. "It's no good you goin' off with them trollops during tha day and now 'can't work'. Well, there's one less of 'em than there used ta be. Since that Nancy twat got herself killed. But you knows that already, I supppose. You with her last night?"

"No, I wasn't," He could feel himself getting angry, and the blood started rising in his head. "I want to keep working here, and thought this was a viable solution."

"Viable, ya say." Mr. McGrey says. "Lemme tell you about 'viable', lad. If ya can't work during tha day, then ya can't work here no more."

"We'll see." Says Charlie, vision red and mouth almost open. He's about to leap across the door, when he is stopped by an invisible... something.

"What ya playin' at?" asks McGrey. "Get off then." And he slams the door. Charlie hears him cursing all the way back to his bedroom and the candle light extinguished.

"Now what am I to do for money?" Charlie wonders silently as his vision clears and teeth recede. "McGrey never goes out at night, since his wife passed on two years past. And for some reason, I can't reach him inside his house. Best get on to Mrs. Powers, and sort that situation out."

Chapter 6

CHARLIE AND EVIE

He climbs on Chauncy, tied at the gate, and starts off. His landlord lives a few houses down the lane from Charlie's house. So it's about a two-mile ride back. He wonders if he should go to her house so very late, no doubt she would not even answer the door at "Mid-night and all is well", calls the Cryer. No, better handle that tomorrow. Charlie rides home and into the stables, where he leads his horse to an open stall, removes the saddle and bridle, brushes Chauncy down and puts the riding equipment in its proper cubbies. There are no signs of life there, but still Charlie can see perfectly well, as if it's just an overcast day. He walks up to his house and opens the door.

"*There* you are." Calls a female voice. "Where ya been, love? What's happen ta me? I feel all wonky. And how come tha room's all red-like? Wait... are you kiddin'?" Clearly, Evie realised what Charlie had done to her, and also, it took Evie a lot less time to recover than it did Charlie. She is sat at his table as he comes in. She rises to greet him, now dressed in one of his light blue shirts that only comes to her hips. She doesn't bother to button it right the way down.

"Let me tell you what I know, sweetheart." He says and explains as best he can all he has learnt about they're mutual condition. She looks at him hungrily throughout his explanation her canine teeth clearly elongated.

"So you done this ta me, then, eh?" she asks and pads barefoot across the floor. "I tried ta have something ta eat whilst you were out and was sick straightaway. So have I gotta kill folks ta carry on stayin' alive? That would be bad!!"

"No, Evie, he explains. "I've made an arrangement with Mikey at The Flying Horse to supply me, and probably us, with blood from animals that seem to do the trick. We can stay here during the day. Oh, and by the by, one of your co-workers got herself killed last night, but that'll have to wait."

"Fine," Evie says. "Let's go see Mikey, I'm starvin' and I don' know what ta do about it. And by the by how's it that you're talkin' so proper-like?"

"You were right in one respect, Evie, when you discovered my particular condition: it seems that I took on the qualities of my first day's victims. When I feed, my speech and maths ability get really acute, as Gavin was my very first. You might to know that you being my second, I also have become an Observant. Oh, and if we're going to The Horse, you might need to put something more on. This isn't Coventry and you aren't Lady Godiva, love!!"

"No," she quips. "I don't just show it off, I let 'em play with it as well." and takes off the shirt. "I gotta get somethin ta eat. I can't even think about nothin' else. Not even a good roll. Oh well, guess I wear this again!"

She puts the same blue dress she had on yesterday. He doubts whether the pub will be open, or Mikey being there, but as he and Jenna live upstairs, maybe he could ask for the sustenance and then go.

Together they go to the stable to get Chauncy again. He's just put her away, but it'll make the trip quicker for Evie to get food and save wear and tear on her bare feet. Furthermore, if they were to walk, they might encounter someone and that would definitely be in serious trouble, given Evie's present state. Charlie remembers how he was in that condition just yesterday when he woke up. How desperate he was to feed, how incredibly urgent he felt to get the sanguine liquid that would make the ache go away! He couldn't take a chance that they could get caught killing someone, especially after poor Nancy got it yesterday.

As usual at this time of night, there are some empty carriages stood next to the barn. He can tell Evie is hurting and desperate to feed, maybe even on Chauncy! He's got to get her some blood and fast. Moving with incredible speed, Charlie grabs the bridle, puts it around his horse's head and leads him to the carriage. He places the straps around Chauncy's belly and draws the reigns through the grommets, then collects Evie. The entire process takes less than a minute.

They ride quickly to The Flying Horse, which, as expected is shut. But the window at the apartment above is open, it's been a warm night, so again as expected. "Let's see." Charlie thinks and jumps where he stands. Instantly he is carried up to the ledge of the window, where he sees Mikey and Jenna, naked on the bed, fast asleep. Charlie starts to enter the window, but, like at Old Man McGrey's, he can't. Something invisible is preventing him going in. Several times he tries different things: holding his breath, as if that would do any good; putting his head down and ramming at the open window space; kicking at the air, but nothing he tries will allow him to proceed. His keen sence of observation that he's inherited form Evie allows him to smell that they have recently had sex.

"Mikey?" Charlie whispers loudly, but Mikey sleeps on. "Mikey!!" louder he whispers, but Mikey merely rolls over still fast asleep. "Ya pratt! Will ya wake up?" Charlie says almost saying it out loud. Third time lucky, eh? Mikey stirs, and looks dreamily across the room to where Charlie is stood in the window.

"What you doin' here, then." He whispers. "Jenna and I had our date night, and are asleep. Now get out of here before she wakes up!"

"I can't, Evie is here, she's... well, like me." Charlie explains, quietly. "She's just awake now and desperate to get some blood. We need to come into the pub and get some."

"I ain't got none." Mikey reples. "Ya gotta wait till tomorrow."

Charlie turns to go.

"Oi, just a mo," Mikey whispers loudly. "I *have* got a little, from the chicken we had last night. Come on in."

"I can't for some reason." Charlie says. "Look." And steps through the open window and into Mikey's bedroom falling on his way into the room. "What!?"

The sound wakes Jenna up. "What the fuck you doin' here at this time o' night?" she screams. "Ger out of here!!" And drags the sheet on the bed over her nude body. Charlie notices cuts on her wrists as she does.

"We're just going now, love." Mikey says quickly, as he pulls his trousers on and takes Charlie by the arm leading him out of the room.

"You better be back here, or you can sleep with *him*!!!" Jenna shouts at Mikey.

"Come on," he says to Charlie. "we better get this over with."

They go downstairs where Evie is waiting, pacing anxiously. As Mikey opens the door, she leaps on him, wild eyes red with hunger, and fangs bared at his neck. It takes all Charlie's strength to get her off Mikey.

"You better get that chicken blood now!" he says, holding her down. She is wildly thrashing on the floor, scratching at Charlie desperately. "Lemme go! Lemme go!" she screams.

Mikey runs to the kitchen, and finds the covered small pot where he put the chicken blood. There's about a cupful in the bottom of the pot. He was saving it for an emergency for Charlie… guess this fits. Alongside, the blood is another pot containing the kidney and liver that he was going to cook up for his patrons the next day. He brings that and the blood up to the front where Evie is still struggling against Charlie's restraining her.

At the sight of the giblets, Evie calms down, but her eyes and fangs are still evidence of her uncompromising urge. Mikey drops the liver and kidney on the floor, which Evie gobbles up unabashedly. Then he gives her the pot of blood, which she grabs out of his hands and pours down her throat. At once, her fangs recede and her eyes go back to their normal bright green hue.

"Thank you, Mikey," she says in a sultry voice. "I'm still famished, but that'll do fer now." She gets up and straightens her dress.

Charlie gets up and his claw marks from Evie have already healed themselves.

"So," Evie says to Mikey. "Charlie says that someone got killed tha other night. Who died, then?"

"It were Nancy." Says Mikey. "The watchman found 'er in the alley off of Fink Hill Street. Throat were tore out, what I here."

"Any idea who could have done such a thing?" Charlie asked.

"Nope. Ain't got no idea." Mikey answered. "Nor even Constable Waterstone, and he's like you Evie, an Observant. And the best I ever seen. Find a tick off a sheep's arse wiffout mussing tha wool, he can."

"I'll bet Evie could give him a right go." Says Charlie. "And me, now."

"Maybe, mate, maybe." Admitted Mikey.

"Mikey!" It's Jenna shouting from the top of the stair. "You comin' back or stayin' down there?"

"Look, you lot," Mikey says to Evie and Charlie, "ya better be off. Maybe a second… date if I can get back in a dosh." And sees them out of the pub. Outside, they listen to him running up the stairs back to his bedroom. Then hears Jenna shriek as the bed creaks. Mikey must have tackled her onto it.

"Let's be on back home, love." says Charlie. "We can have a bit of a chin wag there and leave these two alone."

They climb into the carriage and Charlie snaps the reigns getting Chauncy headed back to the cottage.

Chapter 7

SORTING IT OUT

"Who d'ya think done it then, love?" asks Evie.

"Done what?" Charlie responds.

"Off'ed dear Nancy." says Evie. "But, I can't hardly think o' that now, I'm still starved."

"That's me as well, sweetheart." Charlie says.

"There you are," remarks Evie. "Now ya sound more like your own self."

Charlie tells her "It happens when I get hungry. And somthin' else, as well. I lose my powers. Or at least they're nor as good. And, like you, my eyes go all crimsonny and my front teeth get big n' sharp."

They ride on east, past Charlie's house, then turn left onto Cow Lane and carry on till they come to the outskirts of town and Landsdowne's Sheep Farm. It's now half-past three and the whole town is asleep. No one will know. The couple get out of the carriage, and tie up Chauncy to a post in the fence. In one swift move, they vault the hedgerows into the field, both of them insatiably hungry at this point and select a proper victim for tonight's slaughter. Charlie and Evie pounce upon their prey and sink their teeth into the necks of the two unsuspecting sheep. They drink deeply and at once, the eyes of the predatory couple can see normally, and their canine teeth are back to their regular lengths as the sheep, pelts stained with blood from the two puncture wounds at the neck, fall to the ground, dead and drained.

"We need to start back to mine before dawn, you don't want to see what happens when you go out into the sunlight, Evie." Charlie explains as they untie Chauncy and climb back into the carriage. "It isn't a pleasant experience, I can tell you."

Evie asks "Does it hurt?"

"You have no idea." He tells her. "I'm just wondering why I couldn't go into Mikey's until he said 'Come on in'? Must be another one of those things we going to have to get used to. Oh, and Evie, where do you live, sweetheart?"

"I live on tha first floor of a box of flats on High Pavement, just above tha cobbler's." She explains. "It's not big and I share ut with a couple o' other girls. But if ya want me ta, I can move in with ya. Might make our lot in life a bit simpler."

Charlie announces, "Yes, I think that's the best solution. Maybe tomorrow night, we can get your things, then, darlin'. The sun will be up in about an hour and we'd best get inside before then.

"So, we gonna be together from now on, then, love?" and she winks a smile at Charlie.

"I would say so. But we also have to figure out how to pay Mrs. Powers, my landlord, for the rent fee. I went to Mr. McGrey at the mill and he said owing that I am unable to work during the day, I have no position there. I don't know how we're going to suss it out."

"Maybe I can lift some purses and see what I can get." Evie suggests.

"No. And if you get caught, that would just draw unwanted attention to us and our... condition" He says.

"I can always go back to rollin' drunk lads at Tha Horse. I'll need me outfits of course. Everyone knows I'm just a slag, so if I go back to it, no one's tha wiser, yeah?"

"At the first thought, it's not a bad idea." Charlie says. "But when we get randy, it's the same as when we get hungry. Red vision, fangs come out, and we have to have the person. Badly."

"Sounds all right ta me." Evie says laughingly.

"That's fine, but what if it leads to that other passion?" he asks. "How would we explain another murder in *this* small town? And we would *have* to be questioned about the Nancy's as well?"

They hastily continue the three-mile ride back to Charlie's cottage.

"As to your question before, there are lots of people that had it out for tarts in general, no offence." Charlie stated matter-of-factly. "And even some for Nancy herself. Could be

a lot of folks from town. It'd be a shorter list to see who couldn't have done it."

"No offence taken, love." Evie replies. "Yeah, I was thinkin' tha same thing. But if we could find out who dunnit, there might be a reward innit fer us! That might solve some of our money problems, yeah?"

"I suppose it just might, Evie."

Upon arriving back at the stable, they quickly put Chauncy back into his stall and the equipment away. Mr Firthe isn't up yet, or at least he's not in the stables. The vampyric couple quickly glide inside the front door just as the first rays of the sun appear above the horizon and they close the door behind them.

Once inside, they move affectionately through the front room, with their eyes never leaving each other. Evie undoes the clasp at the waist, whilst Charlie has a bit more to remove, dropping his clothes bit by bit along the way until he's as naked she and they silently approach the bed. They kiss passionately and fall together, entwining their bodies around and between each other. Charlie separates and sits on his knees between her legs, his organ large and erect in front of him. Evie is lying back on his pillows looking at Charlie wantonly. He grasps Evie's feet and holds them shoulder width apart. She reaches down and grasps him in her tiny, but now strong hands.

"Come on, then." She demands. "Give it to me!" and pulls him into her all the way up to his hip as she moans in delight, both of their canines in full view. As he continues plunging into her, they both growl and snarl, rolling over and over each other. They have vehement sex and tear at each other's skin animalistically with their finger nails and teeth. Charlie's passion matches Evie's; another of his newly-acquired gift from her. He now sees why she is in the trade she is. Their repeated mutual orgasms are demonstrated by the erotic cries and shrieks emanating from each of their throats. Despite the windows and curtains being shut and drawn, the neighbours have heard the sounds of their passion over their morning meals.

After the love battle has commenced an hour later, they collapse onto their backs, and lie completely still with arms crossed over their chests and they close their eyes. Neither of them is breathing at all but somehow the sleep is reviving their psyches for the evening ahead.

Chapter 8

CONSTABLE WATERSTONE

Nancy's dead body is under a draped cloth smeared with blood at the rear room of Boyle's Butcher's shop at the far west end of Back Side. It's just after noon on Sunday and the body has been lying there since Friday evening. It's a hot day, thirty-two degrees according to the new Centigrade thermometer, hanging out a rear window. The town has been so much abuzz with the horrible crime, that it's been all Constable Waterstone can do to keep calm. Rumours about killer dogs, wolves, and werewolves are rampant throughout the town. There is also speculation about an angry customer of Nancy's that didn't receive whatever services he paid for. But knowing Nancy as the town did, that conjecture seemed way off the mark.

The door to Boyle's Butcher Shoppe opens and a large man in a navy blue jacket, trousers, stockings and tricorner, with an official badge attached, enters to the ring of the bell attached to the door. His long black hair behind in a pony tail, tied with a navy blue ribbon and his trimmed and twirled mustache connected with a thin hairline to the growth on his chin.

"Hallo, Constable." Said Mr. Boyle in his Irish brogue. He's a stocky man with bright red hair and beard, dressed in tan coloured shirt and dark brown trousers with an apron splattered with blood.

He had come from Ireland a few years ago and settled in to become the town's favourite butcher's. "Ya ready ta take the tart out of my shoppe?"

"She's the victim of a vicious crime, Mr. Boyle," corrects the constable. "I need to do a formal examination of her to determine 'ow she was done in."

"Formal examination?" exclaims Mr Boyle. "Her throat's been torn out. How much more formal can ya get?"

"I've sent word fer a doctor from London to come up and examine her proper." He explains. "There's something that I do know already, Mr. Boyle, but I'm not a doctor, am I? From what I hear, he's some sort of expert on sortin' out wounds. Something ta do with tha blood, I dunno."

"When's he supposed ta be here, then?" asks Mr. Boyle, thickly.

The constable explained, "Hopin' ta hear back from him by Monday and maybe he can come up sommat next week. Me, I just wanned 'a check tha body again, in case I missed a'owit."

"Well, she's still back there," joked Mr. Boyle, "ain't figured she'd got up and left. Come on, let's see the girl."

The butcher leads Constable Waterstone behind the counter and through the long black curtain to where the dead animals are kept for sale to customers. Mr. Waterstone is so tall that he has to bend at the waist in order to get through the doorway to the back area. Up on the shelf are several covered pots. Easily missed by the normal passerby, but certainly not for an Observant.

"What's in them pots, Mr. Boyle, sir?" asks Constable Waterstone. "Spices fer tha meat?"

"Nah, constable," answers Mr. Boyle, "that there's blood from me animals. Use it for me blood pudding, as ya know. But just tha other day, Mikey Whealan at The Flying Horse assed me ta keep a couple a pots fer 'im. Dunno what he wants it fer. Maybe his missus is tryin' ta compete with me mum's recipe. Good luck on that score, I say."

"Perhaps, but why so much," asks the constable, "Can' see *that* much blood puddin', even fer a pub."

"Dunno, constable, sir, he asked, so I did," explained the butcher. "I can't use it all. I usually jus't put it in tha feed fer tha pigs."

"Maybe I should pay a visit to The Flying Horse after this." Said Constable Waterstone. "See what I can see. Speaking o' which."

They arrive at Nancy's covered body. Constable Waterstone throws the blood stained sheet off of her.

"Why she naked?" he asks the butcher.

"Taught that's tha way ya wanted it, sir." Is his reply.

Without looking around, Constable Waterstone asks, "Are those her clothes under there, then? I'd like to see 'em in a bit." And the constable looks carefully at the gaping wound on her neck. "I see. It's like this, is it? See this?"

"'Course, it's the wolf bite that killed her." replied the butcher.

"No, not a wolf bite, that's what they wanst ya ta think; whoever done this." Explained Constable Waterstone. "It's actually a... well, something else. Now about them clothes?"

"Here they are, sir." And Mr. Boyle produces the box from underneath the table. "Can I get ya something ta drink, sir? Ya look heated in that outfit. And it *is* mithring out there."

"Yes, thank you my good man." Says the large officer, and lays out the clothes on the floor next to the table, He kneels down, takes off his cap and carries on inspecting them as Mr. Boyle grabs a glass and heads out back to his well. "Hmm. This is interesting." He says as Mr. Boyle returns with the water. "Have you tweezers, Mr. Boyle?"

Mr. Boyle leaves the glass on the table next to Nancy's body and goes to fetch the tweezers. Constable Waterstone continues surveying the prostitute's clothes. Mr. Boyle returns with the tweezers and hands them to the constable who's just finishing the glass of water.

"Thank you, Mr. Boyle." Says Constable Waterstone and he picks something minute from the blood-stained sheer white blouse with the tweezers. "May I have a small pot that you usually put spices in? Or a small glass?" he asks. Quickly Mr. Boyle takes a tiny juice glass from a cupboard and brings it to the constable. He takes what he found, opens the tweezers and places it in the glass. "This could be useful. Best get some more o' them glasses, mate." And he continues looking over the blouse and blue print skirt. He takes the tweezers, and picks several more small things from the clothing and puts them in separate glasses. "Please hold onto these fer me, Mr. Boyle, I'll be around later to collect 'em. Now, I'd best go on over ta The Horse, an' see what they say about all this blood."

The pair of men walk to the front of the butcher shop. "Cheers, Mr. Boyle," the constable says as he leaves.

"Cheers, constable. Good luck to ya, sir!" answers Mr. Boyle from behind the counter.

The walk from the butcher's to the pub took Constable Waterstone five minutes and he was thinking all along the way about what he found on Nancy's body and clothes. He arrives and pushes open the door. Mikey is at the far end of the bar, pulling pints for two gents.

"Hallo, constable," Mikey calls. "be right with ya."

"No hurry, Mikey." The constable replies and takes off his cap, which he puts under his arm.

"Now, mate, you ok?" Mikey asks.

"Yeah, you?" Constable Waterstone answers.

"Fine, mate, fine. Get ya a pint?"

"I'll have a bitter, please. Also got some questions ta ask ya, if that's all right."

"No worries, gov. I'll get that pint fer ya then we can have a chin wag."

Mikey pulls a full pint of beer from the tap and returns with it to Waterstone.

"So, how can I help ya, conatable?"

"Was just over ta Boyle's Butcher's and wuz wonderin'... why do ya need so much blood from him. Seems a lot fer just makin' blood pudding. Everything all right?" asked the constable taking a large gulp of beer.

"Um, yeah, everything's great. I, um, need the, uh, blood fer..."

"He asked fer me." says Jenna, emerging from behind the curtain that leads to the back. "I need it fer lots of recipes. Mind, I don't tell a lot of folks, but I do. Even in tha gravy, tha pie crusts, tha bread. It's recipes I got from me mum, I ain't used 'em cause I ain't never had all ths blood before. Bur I asked Mikey and he asked Boyle and there it is, constable."

"That the way of it, then, Mikey?" asks the constable, taking another gulp.

"Er, yeah, it's wot she says," he says, "I was sworn ta secrecy, mate. Sorry."

"Well that sorts it, then, many thanks. I'll finish this and be on me way. this is a nice pint, Mikey, thank you."

"It's me uncle's brewery up in Sherwood." Mikey explains. "Do ya like it, then?"

"I do" confirms the constable, "Does *this* have that blood in it?"

Jenna and Mikey glance at each other, suspiciously, "Course not!" the barman says. "Don't be daft, sir. Who would put blood in the beer?" and they both laugh as Jenna leaves quickly to go to the back again as Constable Waterstone finishes his pint and uneventfully leaves the pub, heading back home.

Chapter 9

CHARLIE INSPECTS THE BODY

It's well past eleven o'clock when Charlie and Evie rise from their bed. They dress in silence and knowingly decide that they need to go to Evie's flat and bring her things to Charlie's cottage. But first, the Flying Horse and nourishment as the blood-thirsty couple are both famished.

Charlie is attired in a charcoal grey overcoat, trousers and tricorner with claret shirt, scarf, and stockings. Evie is in the only clothes she has, the same blue kit. They collect Chauncy and carriage from the stables.

"Oi there," came a voice. It's Mr. Firthe. "Can I have tha stable fee then, mate?"

"Of course," Charlie hisses. "Here is tha three quid I owe you, my good sir. Now we *have* ta get on our way!"

"I *need* ta feed!!" Evie whispers to him. "Lemme *have* him!" she begs.

"No, my dear." he whispers back. "We have ta get ta Tha Horse, now. Mikey's got our food all ready... he'd better had done."

Mr. Firthe looked very confused by the whispered conversation.

"What you on about?" he asked.

"Nothin'," Charlie responded behind his hand over his mouth, which had his canine teeth protruding menacingly. "Not ta be rude, but, we *have* ta go, mate. We can chat soon, yeah?" and snaps the reigns getting Chauncy running as Evie practically climbs over him to get to Mr. Firthe. She looks longingly behind her toward him as they ride off.

As they ride to the pub, her hand never leaves his lap, whilst her other hand is moving inside the slit in her dress.

"Later, my love, later." Charlie tells her. They pull up to the back of the pub and both jump down silently. Charlie, eyes crimson with need, ties Chauncy up to the railing whilst Evie hurries inside. She opens the back door and encounters Jenna washing dinner dishes.

"Where? Where!" Evie demands. Her eyes are bright red, her canine teeth fully elongated as her need is virtually insatiable. She is ready to feed on Jenna if needs be, especially if she doesn't give her the blood she requires so desperately in short order.

"Hang on, there, my fine lady," Jenna replies deliberately slowly. "all... in... good... time." She wipes her hands on the towel at her waist and slowly moves across the room to the shelf where the seven covered blood-pots are located. After surveying the group, she selects one and pulls it down, removes the cover, places it in the sink and hands the pot to Evie, who notices scratches on her wrist.

"Now mind ya don't swallow too fast... ya don't wanna choke. Wha't a shame *tha't* would be. Can't imagine a world with one less blood-suckin' tart in it." she says dripping with sarcasm.

Charlie enters the room, as desperate as Evie, but not willing to do Jenna in, not just yet. Evie, drinking the contents of the pot, lifts her head slightly and points to the shelf holding the covered pots. Charlie pushes past Jenna and grabs one of the pots. He tosses the cover away and it smashes on the basin.

"Oi, what ya doin'?" Jenna yells as Charlie continues drinking thirstily. "Just got all the glass outta this cut, so I don't want another one, thank you very much."

Evie is done drinking her pot, which she hands to Jennna and moves back to the shelf for a second helping. There's blood dripping from the corners of her mouth, but she is unconcerned with that now. Her eyes have calmed down a bit and her teeth are not as extended as they had been, but her hunger is still acute. She removes the cover, places it back on the shelf, and drinks eagerly again.

"Well, at least the trallop knows how ta treat someone else's proerty." Jenna says as Charlie moves silently over to the shelf again and takes down a second pot, this time removing the cover and placing it in the sink, as he drinks.

They both have finished their "meal" and now turn to Jenna.

"So, you ok?" Charlie asks her.

"Yeah, you lot?" she replies. "Just wanna let ya know that the constabulary's been here today, askin' about tha blood fer you lot. Lied for you two, me Mikey and I did. So you should be a little thankful, is all. Now, Charlie, you owe me two shillings for tha cover, mate. And don't ya be pushin' me neither, or you can just forget about us keepin' all this… blood. Got some beef liver, if ya want 'em." Tossing her head toward the root cellar and the couple head off. "On a covered plate in there, they are."

Charlie and Evie find the sandwiched plates concealing the organ meat. He takes a knife, cuts the meat in half and passes the plate to her. She takes the larger half, of course, and eats it deliciously whilst Charlie consumes the rest. Their faces revert completely back to normal after finishing the liver. They bring the empty plates out of the root cellar and hand them to Jenna, still doing dishes at the sink, now washing the pots and covers previously holding its gory contents.

"Thank you, Jenna," says Evie. "I know you don't like tarts like me even before I got turned. And I can't imagine ya liking me much more now, so we appreciate ya doin' this for us."

"Look," Janna tells her. "I ain't doin' this fer you. I'm doin' it 'cause Mikey asked me ta. I love 'im and havin' you twats hangin' around the pub, makes temptation for any man; no less my Mikey. So, no, I hate all you lot, if ya still on about what ya used ta be, that is, my dear. Now, I think you're just pathetic and sad." Jenna practically sneers as she speaks to Evie, especially when it comes to prostitutes making The Flying Horse their habitat.

"Well, Jenna, many thanks again," Charlie tells her. "We do have errands to run this evening, but before we go, how did Constable Waterstone find out about the blood?"

"He was over Boyle's Butcher's lookin' at that dead whore, Nancy, when ee seen them pots. So Mikey 'n' me made up a tale about usin' the blood fer recipes! I hope he bought it." she told them.

"Did he find anything'? With Nancy I mean?" Charlie asks.

"I dunno," Jenna says. "I don't think he would have said if he did."

"He say anything about any type of reward fer findin' out who done it?" Evie asks.

"Nah, he ain't said nothin'." Jenna said.

"Well, we're gonna have a look ourselves and see what we can find." Charlie explained.

"I'm sure he don't need tha help of tha pair of ya what can't go out in tha daylight and kills people, so's they can live." Jenna states.

"I think we *can* help." Charlie states in return. "Maybe we can spot things that he might have missed."

"Missed?" declares Jenna. "He's an Observant, ya pillock! He sees things that most folks don't even know's there."

"Evie's an Observant as well, which makes me an Observant... by extension." Charlie explained to her, motioning over to his partner. "And as they say, the more eyes looking at a problem, the easier it is to solve."

"What *you* gonna find, then?" Jenna asks the pair.

"Won't know until we look, will we?" Evie sneerily states back.

"S'ppose not", Jenna sneers back. "Well, best be on your way, then, as ya said. So tarrah, then." It was obviously time for them to leave.

"Right you are," Evie says and the pair head for the back door.

"Say hello and tarrah ta Mike fer us, yeah?" Evie calls back, tauntingly

"I'll say so fer Charlie, bur not fer you, ya slag-bag." Jenna calls out. "And you leave my Mikey alone, ya know what's good fer ya."

"You shouldn't have let her on like that." Charlie chided her as they climb aboard the carriage. "She's actually can make life awfully difficult for us if she wants to."

"Make life difficult fer her, I will, she keeps this up." Evie says while they start out toward Boyle's.

"Mid-night and all is well!" the crier calls out.

"The shop will be closed, but I know where Boyle keeps the key to the back door," Charlie tells her.

They park the carriage at the back of the shop and Charlie runs his hand along the jamb above the door, coming down with the key in his hand. He opens the door and the two of them enter the establishment. There's a smell of meat in the room and hanging in the large walk-in root cellar are the carcasses of a steer and a sheep. Underneath each corpse is a large bowl containing the blood of each animal. There are wrapped meat portions awaiting customers in the morning. The scene is added to by one butcher-block table upon which is the blood-soaked sheet covering Nancy's corpse. On a shelf in a far corner, just outside the root cellar are the glasses containing the bits of evidence removed from her clothing by Constable Waterstone. Charlie removes the sheet from Nancy's body.

"Quite a nasty cut." Charlie says.

"That looks a wolf bite all right." Evie states certainly. "But, look, what's this, under her finger nails? Looks like a bit of skin. Must a scratched the killer, yeah?"

"That's what I was just thinking." Charlie tells her. "These look interesting." And he moves toward the root cellar again. Charlie takes town and examines the three glasses that Constable Waterstone put the items. There's small hairs in one, which he looks at, passes to Evie, then replaces on the shelf. He repeats this task with the other two glasses and notices in another, there are tiny bits of flour, and in the third, metal shards.

"Maybe tha wolf worked at the blacksmith," joked Evie.

"Maybe," he joked back. "Gives us food for thought, anyway. Well, now we know what Waterstone does. I'm thinking there's something we can definitely do here, sweetheart."

"Can I help you lot?" is the deep calling voice of Watchman Masterson, holding a lantern aloft. "How d'ya get in here, then?"

"Butcher Boyle gave us a key," lied Charlie, holding it up. "We were just looking for something to eat this late at night, and we knew he wasn't here."

"Charlie... is that you?" Masterson asks. "didn't see it were *you*, mate, it bein' so dark in here and all."

"Yes, Bill, it's me. And Evie as well." He answers.

"Oh, hiya, Evie, you all right?" he says to her. "Oh, oh, I get it. On fer a li'l roll-around are ya? Well, why don't ya take her on home, then. I'm sure you'd be more comfy there than in *this* place with 'er lyin' here."

"As I said, Bill, we were hungry before we got to it, and Boyle gave me the key, so we just stopped in for a bite."

"Ok, well, lock up after ya done, then, you two." He reminds the pair. "Had some kids breakin' into places and breakin' stuff, so tha town's got me walkin' around makin' sure places were safe."

"I wanted ta eat before I got ta... eat." she jokes to the Watchman, patting her crotch.

"You take it easy on him now, Evie." the watchman reminded her. "He's gotta work in tha morning."

"No worries, Watchman." she tells him. "I'll still have some if *you* want."

"Nah, that's all right, love" he laughs. "Gotta a lot of work meself ya see. I *am* a Watchman, ya know. Well, tarrah, then, you two. Don't do anything I wouldn't" And laughs loudly as he heads out the back door, returning the room to total darkness.

Chapter 10

EVIE'S FLAT

Charlie and Eie return to the carriage, pots in each arm, untie Chauncy and climb aboard the carriage. They ride from the back of the butcher's onto the Fink Hill Road, past the Flying Horse, the other businesses on the main road. As they pass the alley where Nancy was killed, Charlie comments to Evie, "We should have a look-see around here as well, darlin'."

"That's a good idea." she answers, seductively.

They round the corner onto High Pavement Street. The cobbler's shop is halfway down the street, so Charlie pulls the carriage up to the railing in front of the front door.

"Tha light's on in tha flat so someon's 'ayre, you can come on up if ya wanna," Evie tells him and lightly jumps down to the ground. She turns the latch and pushes open the front door. Charlie also jumps silently to the ground and follows her inside after tying Chauncy up to the rail. They ascend the stair to the first floor landing and turn to the door with the number 13 on it. She takes out the key from a pocket in her dress, puts it into the lock and opens the door to the flat. The candle-light illuminates the front room slightly. There are beds against three walls all un-made with clothes strewn all over them and falling out of the wardrobe stood tight next to each one.

To the right is a table with mats in three places and plates, glasses, utensils, and cups in the sink against the unoccupied wall. There is on one at home now, as the other girls are all working at one of the pubs in town.

"That one's mine." Evie instructs and points to the bed and wardrobe against the south wall. "I can get my things if ya want, but we can use the table cloth in my wardrobe to wrap tha things in. Thanks fer ya help, by tha way. Appreciate it."

Charlie pulls down the tablecloth and spreads it out on the floor. Then, he begins collecting the clothes from the wardrobe and bed, placing them on the spread.

"Gotta get outta *these* things." Evie tells him. "Been wearin' 'em fer two days an' they're startin' ta reek. I can smell me own fanny and I ain't had my perfumes." She undoes the clasp and the dress falls to the floor. She pads silently across the room next to him and puts her arm around his neck and presses her naked body against him, gently kissing his wounds. 'Wanna have a good ole roll here fer tha last time, or do ya wanna wait till we get ta yours... ours...whatever ya wanna call it?"

"If we're gonna have a go here, we're gonna have ta feed again." He is clearly aroused and can hear himself speaking in his normal dialect. His eyes feel hot and teeth are not the only things starting to protrude again. "Good job we got them pots in the back at tha carriage, yeah?" He kisses Evie, pulls of his jacket and begins unbuttoning his waistcoat. She anxiously unties his trousers, pulling them down around his feet, then kneels in front of him, taking his organ into her mouth. He moans as he continuous disrobing. He looks down at her and sees her eyes red and enflamed but thirsty and lustful all at the same time. Her red hair thrown all about her face and back as she continues her oral manipulations. Charlie is naked now except for the trousers around his feet and the stockings covering his calf. Evie releases her hold in him, allowing him to remove the rest of his attire. Once completely naked, he grabs Evie, who squeals in delight as he throws her on the bed, legs splayed apart, her hands immediately go to her bits, which she separates for his inspection. It's wet, as she inserts two fingers, moaning and snarling in anticipation, "Come on, lover, give us another go!" She barks at him, teeth completely enlarged and shiny with saliva. Eyes also red with passion, blood pounding in his temples and groin, Charlie mounts her, plunging himself into her again and again. The pair are snarling, growling, and thrashing each other as they furiously make love on the bed and the floor.

It's nearly two in the morning before Charlie and Evie collect themselves and, knowing no one in her neighbourhood is awake at that time, they run down to the carriage, each taking a pot of blood and draining their contents in one long draught. Afterwards, the couple return upstairs, collect Evie's belongings and put them in the rear of the carriage.

"Clearly, we only have one pot left for tomorrow evening's activity." Charlie informs her.

"We had better get on to that alley, if we're going, then." Evie states. "I wanna get a look at where poor Nancy were done in."

Untying Chauncy, they set off in they came, their carriage full of clothes, bed clothes, and other miscellaneous items of Evie's tied up in the tablecloth along with the two empty and one remaining pot of their sustenance.

They arrive at the alley and tie the carriage up to the post just at the entrance. Although the street is lit from the lamp every few metres, the alley, bar the inside foot or so, is in complete darkness; however, the couple's vision is clear.

"Let's have at it then, my dear," says Charlie and he moves to the west side of the alley, whilst Evie begins her search for evidence on the eastern side. There's blood, beer and vomit on the walls and ground of the alley as they look for clues.

"Oi, love," Evie asks, "how we gonna know what's from the murder and what's just here normal-like?"

"I have a feeling we'll know, my dear." Charlie answers. "Just use your Observant skills and it should be fine."

As if on cue and about five metres into the alley, Charlie comes upon a pool of dried blood on the wall and ground in the alley that could only come from extensive damage.

"It's over here, Evie," Charlie calls.

Evie crosses the alleyway to where Charlie is stood.

"Tha constable and watchman have probably been over this area already." Evie says. "But, that watchman is as hopeless as shite. Oi, what's this?"

She reaches down and picks up a shard of glass.

"That looks like it came from a glass from the pub. See the lipstick around the rim."

"'Course I seen it, I ain't bloody blind ya know. And what about this, then?" she asks, and nods her head toward the ground. "What ya think about them, then, love?" pointing out multiple sets of footprints on the ground both adjacent to and on top of the pool of dried blood.

"I noticed them as well, but they could be something or not, darlin'," he answers. "You know, it could be anyone's footprints, not necessarily the killer."

"If that's so, then why they on *top* o' the puddle, then, sweetheart." She asks. "This ain't exactly a busy road, is it? And, all the shoes they come from was only two types. Ya see, that one with tha pointy heel?"

"Yes," he says.

"That one there's poor Nancy's." she explains.

"How do ya know that?" he asks her.

"I was with her when she bought 'em." Evie tells him. "Was a new type from the cobbler's downstairs, they were. She seen 'em in tha window and just *had* ta have 'em. He told her they was from Paris. Ooh la-la." And rolls her eyes and shakes her head in mock enthusiasm, her long hair swishing this way and that.

"All right." He answers, his customary Nottingham dialect beginning to come to the fore. "Now them other ones. What ya make of them? Look like work boots ta me."

"Yeah, they do," she confirms. "But, they're about tha same size as poor Nancy's, ain't they? Could be a short bloke or a bird, couldn't they?"

"My thoughts exactly." Charlie tells her. "Better get some more ta eat, love, I can feel tha hunger come on me again." as he feels his canine teeth beginning to grow again.

"That's me as well," Evie agrees. "Me eyes are startin' ta burn again as well."

They return to the carriage and share the remaining blood-pot. Whilst not as complete as they might have liked, it was enough to return their sight to its normal keenness and reduce their canines to relatively normal lengths. By now with all their examinations it's four in the morning and the sun will be rising within an hour.

"We'd better head off back home, love." Charlie tells her. "Now that we have what we know, we can start to speak to Constable Waterstone tomorrow evening and see if we can help with his investigation."

The couple climb aboard the carriage after untying Chauncy and take the ride back to Charlie's cottage. They unload Evie's clothes tied up in the table cloth and she takes them into the house. Charlie settles his horse back into his stall as Evie starts unwrapping the cloth and begins to take her belongings out one by one as she awaits her partner. As she thinks of Charlie, she also begins removing her own clothing, putting them into the wardrobe along with the ones she brought.

Evie moves to the doorway. "Come on, Charlie," she calls to him, exposing her naked body. "come and get it, lover, before ya get burnt up!" she jokes.

Charlie runs to the doorway, eager to match her desire. He shuts the door and removes his clothing until he is as naked as she. He kisses her strongly and moves her further inside the cottage. Their sex is as violently passionate as ever. He turns her around and bends her at the waist over the footboard of the bed as looks back at him and growls in anticipation of what is to come. He moves close behind his erection, strong and firm and he growls back at her as she spreads her dainty feet to shoulder-width apart. He enters her from behind and she scratches his chest with her sharp nails. He grasps her breasts and pulls her to him as he fills her completely. This is only the first of many sessions that consume their mutual insatiable lust.

Chapter 11

MRS. POWERS

After a rousing early morning of lovemaking, growling, and snarling, along with hair-pulling, back-scratching and continual position switching, Charlie and Evie collapse into a dead sleep.

Charlie arises at half-past two in the afternoon, much earlier than normal, and wonders why. He's incredibly hungry again, of course, but that never awoke him before sunset since his turning, and that was after five days later. Maybe this was another development in his new condition.

He's startled from his contemplations by a knock at the door.

"Who, is it?" he asks.

"It's me, Charles Butterworth." Calls a hoarse female voice. "Mrs. Powers. Tha lady what keeps a roof over your lazy arse, 'ese days."

"Hold on, love, will ya?" he calls back.

"Love!?" she says, loudly, "Oh, I'll give ya 'love' and 'hold on' too, I will." She chides him through the door as she kicks it in mock aggravation. "You owe me money fer yer rent. An' when am I gonna see some o' that?"

Charlie wraps the sheet around him and opens the door a crack. He stands just inside the doorway in the darkened room and sees the short, stout, older woman that is his landlord stood there, arms folded, in a grey house dress and white apron with a grey kerchief on her mostly ginger hair that halfway has gone grey itself. The day itself is as grey as her kit, and it's raining. Charlie stands at the open door, again in contemplation. Perhaps the lack of sunlight is why he was awakened so early.

"You all right?" she asks him, pushing the door open a little more. "Ya look kinda pale. And what's with your eyes, lad, been cryin'?" Unexpectedly, as the day crosses his face, there's no burning reaction like previously. Again, the lack of sunlight, the blocking of the sun by the rain clouds, has stopped his skin from spontaneously combusting.

"No, I'm fine." he says to her, absentmindedly. "Ya'll have ta ask Ole Man McGrey, he's tha one what pays *me*."

The landlord peers past him through the door where Evie is still in repose, hands crossed over her naked breasts on the bed, red hair splayed on the pillow, but now moving slightly as she begins to awake herself.

"Oh," she scolds him. "I see why ya got no rent fer me! It's them nasty twats ya spend all ya' time with. Why can't ya find a nice girl, instead of them trollops. There's no future with them types. They just want yer money and all they probably spend it on is gin or whiskey. And what kinda person is *that*?"

"Ya right missus, sorry." Says Charlie trying to hide his canine teeth from her view. Her spectacles lay low across her Roman nose. "I'll have tha rent money fer ya tomorrow, then, if that's all right." He assures her.

"So long as ya got it for me tomorrow, then, lad," she tells him. "Otherwise, it's out ya go. An' get rid of that rubbish."

"Thank you, Mrs. Powers." Charlie tells her. "So how ya gettin' on now that yer husband left? Any idea where he gone and when he might be back?"

"Nah," she replies, "and it's good riddance to bad rubbish, I say. So, I will *have* it tomorrow, then." She says, changing the subject.

"I can swear ta it." He says.

"Right," she says back. "And I'll hold ya ta it. Tarrah, then Charles. And get rid o' that." She points at Evie. "And get somethin' done about ya teeth as well, dear. They're 'orrible!"

"Thank you, again. Tarrah." And Charlie shuts the door.

"Who was *that*?" Evie asks from the bed. She's sat holding her knees up to her chest.

"My landlord." he explains to her. "She wants tha ren' money. Told 'er she'll have it tomorrow."

"Oh yeah? And how we suppose ta have *that*, then, love." Evie asks him. "We clearly have the funds ta *pay* 'er, now don't we?"

"Oh, I dunno, love," he sarcastically answers. "Maybe we could have *you* perform your former, special duties, then, yeah?" and he shrugs. "I truly dunno."

"Well, if ya need tha funds… " she says.

"Nah, sweetheart. I was just thinkin'." Charlie says, kindly. "But, we do need three things, we need ta go to Tha Horse, we need ta go see Constable Waterstone, and we need a get a 'tenna' foh Mrs. Powers."

"All right but how can we go out, it ain't night-time." Evie reminds him.

Charlie tells her of what happened when he opened the door to his landlord.

"Here, watch *this*." And he opens the door, still dressed in the sheet. Again, his skin is still intact, without the sun's rays burning him to a crisp.

"Well, this a good thing we live in England then, isn't it." She jokes back. "We must have three-hundred days of rain every year. Hahahaha."

"C'mon, sweetheart, let's get dressed and head off, then." Charlie tells her. "We got a long day ahead, remember? Thought we'd just take Chauncy today."

After dressing in proper rain attire, including a wide-brimmed cap and leather shawl for each of them, they bridle and saddle Chauncy. Evie's shawl is held in place by a brooch in the form of a butterfly whilst Charlie's is a leaf-shaped clasp. Charlie then puts two large leather package carriers on each side of the horse hind side and climbs aboard, Evie climbing up after and right behind him, but in front of the carriers. As they gallop, their hunger is intense. Charlie's vision is so red, that he's very glad Chauncy knows where the pub is located, because he's not sure whether or not he could see the road ahead. He knows that Evie is feeling the same way because her fingernails are digging into his sides very hard, harder than is necessary to hold onto the horse.

They tie Chauncy up outside and rush into the pub, where Mikey is behind the bar chatting up one of the girls. He turns when he sees the dripping wet couple.

"Oi, *you* two, you all right?" he shouts, running over, leaving the brunette in a dark red peasant blouse and skirt stood there by herself. "You two kinda early today, ain't ya." He whispers. "Just got a delivery from Boyle's a few minutes ago, it's back here. C'mon." And he leads the pair to the back room. There are seven blood-pots up on the shelf and they take down one, drink through it quickly and take and drain a second one each.

"We can never say 'thank you' enough, Mikey." Charlie says appreciatively. Charlie notices that Mikey is wearing work boots.

"Well, maybe *I* can show ya how much, yeah?" Evie suggests, taking his hand and putting it inside her shirt to feel her erect nipple.

"Evie, you still got tha itch, then, have ya?" he responds, pulling his hand away. "Don't get me in trouble with Jenna, sweetheart."

"How's *she* gonna get *you* into trouble, eh?" says his wife angrily, who has come up behind him, facing Charlie and Evie. "Ya *better* not get me Mikey into trouble ya slag! Get outta here, and walk tha streets with tha other slags with dirty knees and bums!"

"Well, a' least I ain't let meself go so much she can't see her own shoes." Evie comes back with, looking down at her work boots. It's remarkable to both Evie and Charlie, who is now looking down, and gives her a sideways glance acknowledging their mutual observation, that Jenna and Mikey have feet of roughly the same size.

"That's it, then, dearie," Jenna lets her know, striding up to her, hands on her hips. "Well, you don't have ta come in fer your 'supply' no more, then. And you lot can expect a visit from the law as well, when I get through with them."

"Now, Jenna, they're our mates, love." Mikey tells her. "No sense makin' trouble fer the pair of 'em."

"Oh, you on their side, are ya?" She turns to face her husband. "Well, you can join this pair on tha streets as well, my lovely."

"Look, I never said that, love." Mikey says. "All I said was, if she says she's sorry, maybe we can just go on like before, yeah?" with that he turns to Evie, and gives her a nod toward his wife.

"Sorry, Jenna." Evie says, through gritted teeth, fire in her eyes.

"Jenna, your turn now, sweetheart." Charlie says to her.

Barely audible to Mikey, but crystal clearly to the two vampyres, Jenna whispers "Sorry, Evie," through gritted teeth.

"There." Mikey says to the two women who eye each other viciously, but are not at each others throats... not yet at least. "Isn't that better? Gettin' on just like always."

"Listen, Mikey, we'd best be on our way, I think" Charlie informs him. "We have two more stops to make before it gets too late and we can't see the people we need to."

"That might be a good idea, lad." The barman agrees. "Say g'night, Jenna."

"G'night, Charlie." His wife says deliberately.

Chapter 12

MEETING WITH CONSTABLE WATERSTONE

And with Evie carrying one blood-pot and Charlie the remaining two, the couple pass through the curtain and the busy bar, and push their way out the door to the waiting horse and place two of the pots in the carriers at the back of their ride. They realise that with everything that went on in the pub today, the sun has now set.

"You've got to hold onto this one, love." He tells Evie. She jumps onto Chauncy in one gentle leap, holding onto the pot of liquid. Charlie, seeing her, repeats the feat, landing so gently in the saddle in front of her that the horse doesn't even move a muscle.

"Let's on to the constable's house." Charlie says, giving Chauncy a nudge.

"Five o' tha clock an' all is well." it was the Town Cryer again.

They ride west along the road and turn north onto High Parliament, but instead of turning east back to the cobbler's and Evie's old flat, the turn west and quickly the houses get further apart and the roads less distinct. Charlie brings Chauncy to an easy stop in front of a house on the left where there's a light on in the front room and a round, glass around a candle at the front railing. He dismounts, and ties his horse up to the railing as Evie climbs down, and puts the blood-pot against the inside of the closest rail. Even though now it's teeming down rain, Charlie and Evie have fed, so they don't feel the rain that would normally drenched and perhaps chilled them to the bone.

"You remember, we can' go inside till he invites us, yeah?" she reminds Charlie.

"I know, I've thought about that, darling," he says. "I'm hoping to arrive at an appropriate time."

They go up the path and Charlie knocks at the door, Evie at his side.

"Who is it?" comes a voice from within.

It's Charlie Buttersworth and Evie, Brien, is it too late?" he asks. "We have some information about poor Nancy's death."

"Just a mo," the constable calls back. The couple hear dishes rustling inside the house, and a female voice whispering, "What they doin' here, this time a night? You're not on all day every day, ya know... Fine, hear 'em out and let's finish with dinner." the woman scolds the constable.

"Be right there." He calls to them. "I know, love." He whispers back to the other voice. "I'll sort them out and be right back,ok?" A chair scrapes against the floor and a utensil is placed on a plate.

A second later, the constable opens the door and is standing in front of the drenched pair.

"So, what do you have?" the constable asks.

"We're getting soaked out here, Brien." Charlie says and waits for the response.

"We've just sat down to dinner," Waterstone informs them and hesitates. "But it is hammering down out there... so would you two like to come in?" and moves back away from the doorway.

"Thanks, love." Evie responds and enters first, followed by Charlie. All three stand on the other side of the front room from the dinner table.

"This is Flo, my partner and our children, Emma and Daniel." Constable Waterstone nods in their direction, "and as I said, we were just sat down to dinner. Would you like something?"

"No thank you, Brien," Charlie thanks him. "We just...ate."

"Well, then," Brien asks. "Again, how can I help ya?"

"Evie and I visited both Nancy's body, just like you did." Charlie tells him.

"You did *what* ?" the large man bellows. "You are not suppose' ta *do* that. The good people of Nottingham pay me to perform investigations. And I've asked a scientist from London to come up and inspect the body. If you've disturbed *anything*, I'll have you in irons and put to the gallows!"

"We ain' touched *nothin'*." Evie tells him, with a sneer. "We just looked at her and your glasses with all that stuff in 'em. What *was* that anyway?"

"That, my dear, is known as 'evidence'." Constable Waterstone informs her. "Have you been anywhere else snooping 'round?"

"Yes, we went to the alley off of Fink Hill Street." Charlie informs the constable. "And we think we found something interesting."

"When did you go there?" Waterstone asks.

"Last night," Evie says. "And if ya don't wanna know what we got, no worries, we can do your job. And better than you all right. We can go ta tha mayor if ya want and we can get paid fer everything you do."

"Now, hold there Evie." the constable stops her. "I ain't sayin' that I can't use help on this. I ain't never had a murder before, so if you know anything, I can surely use it. I just didn't want a pair of pillocks wanderin' about and muckin' up tha works, is all. Ok?"

"That's all right constable," Charlie tells him. "Evie is just a little high-strung, Brien, as you know. She just wants to find out what happened."

"Listen, mate," the constable tells the pair. "If you can help me solve this, I'll tell the mayor and he'll either pay you this time or make you another constable, Charlie."

"What about me?" Evie asks. "I ain't exactly wealthy ya know."

"Oh, sorry, Evie, I thought you were a team." Constable Waterstone told her. "The same pay I get for Charlie I'm sure I can get fer you, too, love. Ok?

"That's better." she says, "sorry about before, darlin'," then leaning in and whispering in his ear, "let me make it up to ya, somehow, then."

"I don't think so, Evie," he tells her quietly, then louder, "so what did you find?"

"We think the powder in tha glass might be flour." she lets him know, shrugging.

"That was what I thought as well." he said. "maybe from a cook."

"Did you see the foot tracks by the body?" Charlie asks the detective.

"I did, but couldn't make any conclusion in the darkness," Waterstone answers. "Could you?"

"We think so, love," Evie says.

Charlie adds, "Evie identified one of the shoes as Nancy's, as she bought them with her. The other tracks I knew were from work boots. They were flat, with a slight heel to them."

"Well, that doesn't cut down on the person that might've done it," explains Brien. "Just about everyone in town wears them; both men and women. Listen, tha rain has washed away any trace of evidence from tha alleyway, so what you found out ain't there anymore. I think that's what tha killer wanted. I wanna talk to you two more, but can't right now, in fact I'd better get back to dinner just now."

"No worries, constable," says Evie. "When ya wanna get together again?"

"I'm making my nightly rounds after I eat. So, let's meet over at yours, Charlie, around nine tonight?"

"That would be fine, Brien." Charlie responds. See ya then, mate."

The two then turn to go. "G'night, Flo, it was a pleasure to see you again." says Charlie to the table. "Yeah, missus, g'night, then." Evie adds.

"G'night, you two." Flo calls back as they head out the door.

Chapter 13

A SECOND DEATH

Evie gathers the blood-pot and again jump silently aboard Chauncy. Charlie unties his horse and just as silently jumps into the saddle in front of her. "Well, love, guess that kinda solves our problem with Mrs. Powers, eh?" Evie tells Charlie.

"Yes, for the time being, but..." Suddenly despite the pelting down rain, Charlie and Evie hear the Watchman's whistle blow.

"That came from up ahead, maybe Bearward Lane." Evie says.

Quickly, they speed up toward the direction of the whistle. Evie almost drops the blood-pot cover several times on way, but manages to secure it tightly against her body. Even so, some still splashes out of the pot and onto her white off the shoulder crop top.

"Slow down will ya?" she begs Charlie. "He'll still be there in tha next five minutes, ya know."

"Sorry, love," he says, slowing down slightly. "I jus' wanna find out what's goin' on."

"I know, sweetheart," she agrees, "and maybe there'll be another reward in it fer us. Ya tyhink?"

"That was my thought as well, love," Charlie let her know. "Don't forget we have to get Mrs. Powers five pounds by tomorrow."

They finally arrive where Watchman Msterson's whistle is sounding. Evie was right, he's stood at the entrance to an alleyway on Bearward Lane, whistle to his lips, underneath his enormous moustache.

"Well," he says as they dismount. "Didn't expect to see *you two* here t'night."

"We've just been to Constable Waterstone's when we heard you sound out." Charlie explains, dismounting Chauncy. "What seems to be the difficulty?"

"Got another one, here." Masterson nods into the alley. "Got another murder. Say Evie, ya got somethin' on yer shirt there. Is that beetroot juice, then, love?"

"Yeah," she lies, also dismounting silently. "That's what's in these pots, Billy." And Evie puts the blood-pot on the ground at the other side of the entrance to that alleyway.

"Oh, yeah, well that makes sense." He responds. "I think you know this one, Evie, it's Betsy, another tart, mind me sayin' so."

"No worries, Billy." she says. "Yeah, I knows 'er. We used ta be flatmates, till I moved in with our Charlie, here."

"She's just like tha other one, throat tore out. Can't understand it. Never had nothin' like this before. I hope tha constable can sort it out," the Watchman says. "I can't make no heads nor tails of it."

"You know, our Evie here is also an Observant," Charlie reminds him. "Maybe she can help you out?"

"Ooh, yeah," Masterson agrees eagerly. "What ever you can do ta help, suits me, love. But I don't know what yer gonna see in this rain."

"I'm gonna need Charlie there with me, Billy." She tells him. "He's like my right arm."

"Oh, all right, then you two, go on in. She's about twelve paces inside, I counted 'em!" Masterson informs them proudly. "But it's dead dark in there. You'll need a torch. Here, you can have mine. I'll wait out here for Constable Waterstone. No doubt he's heard my whistle too, but I'll keep on just ta be sure." And Watchman Masterson begins blowing again.

Charlie and Evie go into the pitch-dark alley, but again, given their states, their vision is clear. Sure enough, as the Watchman told them, Betsy's dead form is inside the alley about 12 metres. They look down at her lying on her side with water-drenched blood staining her light yellow low-cut dress. Her throat is indeed torn out, just like Nancy, and in her hand is a glass that probably contained the gin she was drinking.

"Don't move anything yeh," Charlie tells Evie. It's obvious that the scene has increased the hunger of the two vampyres. "I wanna see if there's foot tracks underneath tha body. But let's feed first, yeah?"

"How we gunna do that with tha Watchman out there?" Evie asks him.

"Watch and see, sweetheart." he tells her.

They return to the entrance where the Watchman is still blowing up.

"We need one of them pots, Bill." Charlie tells him. He's glad he left the torch inside the alley next to Betsy's body. That way it's very difficult for the Watchman to see their red eyes and elongated canines. Despite it being dinner time in most homes, a small crowd has gathered outside the alley in response to hearing the whistle.

"What for?" Masterson asks. "Everyone; just clear out. Official business. Go on then. Off ya get."

"We need 'em cause tha beetroot juice inside makes tha blood come out more. And we can see it easier."

"Really!" says the Watchman, eyebrows raised in surprise. Well, I guess ya do learn something everyday. Go on then, do ya need any help? They're heavier than I thought." He said lifting the one on the ground. "Ya sure you can manage, Evie?"

"No worries, Billy." She tells him. "I got a new lease on life, I have." and, winking, she takes the pot from Watchman Masterson's hands. Charlie meanwhile, has taken one of the other pots from the carrier on the back of Chauncy.

"Ya need *two* of 'em?" Masterson asks them, "Go on then. Nothin' ta see here." He says loudly as the crowd starts to disperse too slowly for his liking.

"There's a lot a blood, isn't it?" Evie replies with a thirsty look in her eyes.

"Oh, yeah. You're right". He agrees. "Carry on then" he replies, sounding official.

As soon as they're out of sight, they remove the covers to the blood-pots and consume their contents, as they hear the Watchman whistle start up again.

"Well, that's certainly better, isn't it Evie." Charlie says. "Now let's move the body and see what we can see."

"I do feel better now." She tells him. "C'mon less have at it."

They return to poor Betsy's corpse, and lift her up. There in the mud is the same small hairs that were at Nancy's scene as well as the tell-tale footprints made from work boots.

I wanna see something." Charlie says as the rain continues to fall. He puts his right hand down and spreads his fingers. It covers most of the footprint.

"Evie come here," he instructs her. "Put your hand next to my thumb." She moves close and puts her closed hand next to his spread one. It covers more than the print. "Take two fingers next to it." She does as she is told. This time it's a perfect fit. "We need ta get some measurin' done." She tells him. "This could be worth something important."

It's only as they leave the body, that they realise that the whistle has stopped blowing. As they get to the entrance of the alleyway, they see Constable Waterstone has arrived and is speaking with Masterson. The rain has subsided almost completely as they approach the conversation.

"... and they're inside right now." Masterson tells the constable. "Ooh, sorry, here they are!"

"So what have you discovered, then?" Watersone asks the pair, turning to face them. "Anything of importance?"

"Yeah," Evie replies and looks at Charlie. "Can tell 'em?"

"Of course, Evie, my love." Charlie confirms. "Please continue."

"Well, constable," Evie begins. "We found tha same hairs what were in tha glass of yours at Boyle's. Also, there was work-boot foot-tracks underneath her body. And we even measured 'em! How's *zat* fer dectecin'?"

"Impressive work, you lot." Waterstone concedes. "As I said, I'm gonna be speakin' to tha mayor so you can get some money for yer work here."

"Oi, what about me?" asks the Watchman. "Am I gonna lose out of bein' a Watchman? I did find her, Brien."

"No, this has nothin' ta do with you, Bill." The constable informs him. "You are very valuable ta this town."

"Whew." Masterson says and breathes a sigh in relief. "Thank you, Constable."

"Anything else, Charlie? Evie?" asks the constable.

"Can't think f anything else, Constable." says Evie.

Chapter 14

JENNA'S DILEMMA

"I have one request, Brien." Charlie says brightly. "I was wondering if you could let me borrow, and I do mean borrow, a fiver so Mrs. Powers don' kick us out of the 'ouse."

"I never *lend* money," Waterstone says. "especially ta friends, but, I will *buy* something from you Charlie. Or should I say Evie. I would like to buy take that brooch on your shawl, if it's for sale. Flo's birthday is next week and I have nothin' ta get her."

"Tha's fine, Brien," Evie says. "Can I call you Brien, then, love?" and removes the brooch and undoes the shawl, exposing her ample cleavage barely concealed beneath a low-cut puffy sleeved bright green flowy cotton dress. "It's stop' rainin' anyways." she concludes and hands Waterstone the trinket. "I hope she likes it, as it always brought me good luck. After all, I was wearin' it when I first met Charlie, li'l over year ago, it was. And see what's happened since?"

Constable Waterstone hands the five-pound note to Evie. "Many thanks, Evie. And, yes, I know she will love it. She'd seen one like it in Wilson's Jeweller's and remarked on it. So, thank you. Well, ya've gave something to chew on about this second killin'. And, yes, Brien would be fine."

"Thank you, Brien." Says Charlie. "We've gotta deliver this to my landlord before she has a heart attack."

"Yeah, we gotta be on our way, Brien." Evie chimes in. "Oh, but we also gotta bring those pots back ta Mikey at The Horse'."

"Oh, yes, that's right, he'll be wondering where they are." Charlie adds and starts to head back into the alley to retrieve the two empty blood-pots.

"So, why do you have them?" the constable asks, stopping Charlie in his tracks.

"They was using 'em to see tha blood more clearer." Watchman Masterson answers knowingly. Charlie and Evie look at each other suspiciously as Charlie heads into the alley to finally get the pots and covers.

"I see." says the constable. "Say, are you goin' ta be at your house after yer errands, you two? I'd like to call on you after this. I that's all right."

Charlie and Evie look nervously at each other, wondering if he's going to put them in the nick or worse... There is the situation about Gavin after all.

"Why, yeah," Evie says, hesitatingly. "Though, I can't promise we'll be dressed at tha time," and winks at him.

"Well, Evie, I'm sure you can find *something* to put on when I call on you, even if it's a tea towel!" Waterstone says smilingly.

"Bye, then, Billy," she says to Watchman Masterson, giving him a hug. "Don't work too hard, love. Tha girls at Tha Horse will be lookin' out fer you, darlin'."

"Really?" he says, surprised. "Well, in that case, I'll have ta put on a better kit then... and maybe even take a bath as well!" and puffs out his chest.

"You'll be irresistible, love." Evie tells him and releases her hold as Charlie returns with his contents. He puts one in the empty carrier behind Chauncy and hands the other one to Evie.

"I'll see you lot in about an hour, then." Waterstone reminds them.

"Fine, Brien." Charlie says and climbs aboard the horse and pretends to help Evie up behind him. "Best be off quickly," he whispers to her.

"Yeah," she confirms as they turn the horse around and head to the pub to deposit their empty pots, "especially now." she adds once they're out of sight and holds up a purse full of coins. "I nicked it off Billy." She says proudly. 'It'll get us through things for a couple o' days. Besides, he won't miss it. 'His folks are from royalty, he's related ta something at Tha Castle. How d'ya think he got tha job as Watchman? He *is* kinda thick, ya know. Good heart, but thick."

"Yes, I see." Charlie agrees. "Can't believe he bought that beetroot story, love."

"Thick, like I said." she replies as they arrive at The Flying Horse.

The pair lightly dismount from Chauncy onto the ground.

"Here, give me Bill's purse, love." Charlie instructs Evie. "I'll put all of our funds together, in mine and leave the Watchman's outside here. He'll think he's dropped it on rounds and be grateful that someone's given it him back."

Charlie ties his horse to the rail and takes the empty blood-pot out of its carrier and he and Evie bring their pots into the pub. Mikey sees the two come in from across the bar and rushes over to them.

"C'mon, c'mon, you two," he tells them and rushes them and the pots through the curtain to the back. "From now on, bring 'em in through tha back door, Jenna'll be there ta take tha empty ones and give ya fresh."

He takes two more covered blood-pots off the shelf and placed them on the floor next to Charlie. Meanwhile, his wife stood back arms folded disparagingly, never letting her stare of Evie drop. Evie, with her keen Observant abilities, was certainly aware of her leer.

"Ayup, Jenna," she said without looking at her. "You all right?"

"Fine." The barman's wife tells her, unmoving. "You?" to Charlie

"I'm lovely, dear. I just wanna say, I didn't mean nothin' by chattin' up Mikey, it was just that I had tha scratch on." Evie explained. "Then our Charlie come along. So ya got nothin ta worry about."

"Is that right?" Jenna sneered her reply. "Well, we'll see, won't we, dear."

"Can we go, now, love?" Evie asks Charlie. "We need ta see Mrs. Powers, and get back before Constable Waterstone knocks at tha door."

"No, you're right, Evie, love." Charlie tells her. "Tarrah, then, Mikey, and thank you again, mate." And shakes his hand. "Tarrah, Jenna, love." And he leans over and gives her a hug and kiss on the cheek. "She's right, you know, she's with me now." He whispers in Jenna's ear.

"Two of a kind, eh?" Jenna replies, shaking her head and reluctantly smiling to him, and Charlie and Evie notice that her stance has noticeably relaxed. "Tarrah, then you two." She calls as Mikey leads them out the back door, each of the vampyric pair carrying a newly filled blood-pot.

"She'll be all right." Mikey tells them. "She just needs ta get used ta it. And thank you fer sayin' what ya did, Evie. It'll make the change easier on her."

"Cheers, mate," Charlie calls back. He then puts his pot in the carrier again and Evie, still holding hers, in one move, leaps gently astride Chauncy. Charlie makes the same move, and lands silently atop his horse, who again doesn't move a muscle.

"You'll have ta teach me how ta do that." Mikey says appreciatively as they ride off, waving their good-byes.

"Eight o' tha clock and all is not well!" they hear the Town Cryer.

Chapter 15

THE CONTABLE VISITS

The pair of vampyres ride along the High Pavement road and turn again onto Stoney Street. They ride past Charlie's, and now Evie's, turning right onto Goose Gate to the second small cottage on the right.

"She live here, then, yeah?" Evie asks.

"Yes, and she won't like us being here so late at night." Charlie informs her. "Well, best get this over with, love." And jumps down off of Chauncy, gently touching down on the ground. With Evie still astride Chauncy, blood-pot in her hand, Charlie glides up to the door on the flagstone walkway and knocks.

"Just there," came the female voice behind the door. Then quieter, but loud enough for Charlie to hear clearly, "This time o' night, my goodness!" He hears the latch on the door click and Mrs. Powers, in a dressing gown and nightcap comes to the door, candle in hand. "Charlie? Charlie! What you doin' turnin' up at this time o' night?"

"I have five pounds for you and I wanted to give it you before I forget..." Charlie begins.

"Or spend it on trollers." Mrs. Powers adds as he hands her the note.

"Mrs. Powers, the Reformation *is* over, Cromwell *is* out... permanently, and according to Parliament, we shouldn't look down on anyone... now." Charlie reminded her.

"Thank you for that, Charlie. But not in this house!" she comes back with. "I can say what I want in me own house."

"Well, Evie's with me now, so be nice... or nicer." He teases.

"Well! ain't that nice for ya, Charlie." She tells him sarcastically. "I'll do me best. Anything else?"

"No, just the rent, Mrs. Powers." Charlie says. "We'll be on our way now. G'night."

"G'night, Charlie." She says and just nods toward Evie aboard Chauncy.

"C'mon, Charlie." Evie says after his landlord shuts her door. "I'm not bothered, love. She's just a sour ol' cow since her husband up and left. Let's go back, Waterstone'll be there soon and I need it from you before he gets there." And smiles wickedly at Charlie as he can feel his passion rise again and the blood start to heat in his groin and ears.

Back to Charlie's they ride, Evie dismounts and carries her pot and one of the ones in the carrier inside the cottage as Charlie puts the saddle, bridle, and carrier away, then brushes the Chauncy down before putting him in his stall. He carries the last blood-pot into the house. He just gets inside when Evie jumps out from behind the door on top of his back in a surprise "attack". He lets the pot drop to the floor, reaches behind him, grabs Evie by the hair and throws her to the ground. She's naked, of course and is just about to pounce again when there's a knock at *his* door.

"You decent Evie?" Constable Waterstone calls from behind the closed door.

"I will be in a few, me ducks." She calls back, taking a tea towel from the door of the stove and holding it to her chest, then sits in one of the kitchen chairs with her legs crossed. "C'mon on in, then." she calls to him. The towel barely covers anything, but at least she's wearing something... as she said.

The constable walks in and sees Evie on the chair across the front room.

"I hope I ain't interrupted anything." he says in her direction. "Nice kit. Glad that the Watchman ain't here. He'd be beside himself."

"Don't know why," Evie tells him. "I'm just an ordinary working bird."

"Really? Not quite, love," the constable replies. "Not you nor him. Neither of you are exactly 'ordinary', are ya, sweetheart?"

"What do you mean constable?" Charlie asks him.

"Let's see, all of a sudden you're talkin' all formal, teeth all long-like and her," he nods toward Evie. "she can't keep her clothes on. Not that she ever could, mind, but, now... well... you're vamps ain't ya."

Charlie and Evie look at each other. "Yes", they both say, looking down after a pause.

"So, killed anyone lately?" he asks the couple. "I knew it when I seen them pots in The Horse. Blood puddin'... that *was* good."

"No, we haven't killed anyone, Brien." Charlie says. "We've found, quite by accident that any animal blood will suffice and Mikey is getting us that blood with free deliveries from Boyle's. He's been keepin' 'em in these pots ta bring on home."

"Well, there's tha Charlie we all knows," the constable declares. "Does that happen when ya need blood, then, mate?"

"Yeah," admits Charlie. "And when I get... excited." And looks directly at Evie, who's twirling her tea towel now instead of wearing it and looking devilishly at Charlie. Her eyes are turning pink as well and it is indeed time to feed for the both of them.

"Would you excuse us for a mo, constable?" asks Evie. "It's time fer us. Then we'll have a bit of a chin wag, yeah?"

"Fine, I'll just wait outside, till you're done, then." He informs them. "Don't take too long, I do have ta speak with ya." And he turns and goes through the door.

As soon as the constable has leaves the room, Charlie and Evie each take up a blood-pot and drain their contents completely. Evie wipes her mouth with the tea towel, passes it to Charlie, who wipes his and passes it back to her to use again for whatever covering it makes.

"Many thanks, constable, you may come in now." Charlie says, opening the door. Constable Waterstone comes through the door, surveying the scene and sees Evie sat on the kitchen chair with the tea towel and one foot up on the chair seat. Not that anything was being covered or that she was being discrete by any means.

"Well, everything done now, yeah?" he asks.

"Yes, Brien, we're all done now." Charlie replies and Evie nods in agreement.

"What I wanted ta talk to you about is helpin' me in this investigation," says the constable. "I can see what I can see, but, you... well, you two have other abilities what I don't have. I can do things during tha day, you can do things during tha night. See? That gives us all day every day ta get this thing solved quick so no one else has ta get killed. We can work together, if ya want."

"Well, this is an unexpected turn, Brien." says Charlie, relieved. "We'd be happy to help you with this matter. Now you said that there would be some funds in it for us, yeah?"

"I said I would speak to tha mayor and I will do." Waterstone confirmed. "Now, can I count on you two ta help me? You see, I also have a scientist comin' from London tomorrow. So with you two helpin' and poor Nancy should be solved in no time at all. He's brilliant, what I hear, and I know he can help so long as he don' interfere with what *we're* doin'."

"Yeah," chimed in Evie from the chair. "it'd be a shame ta have anything happen ta him."

"Now, now, we'll have none o' that," said the constable. "Even if he does discover your secret, you two, he's from London and I'm sure he's seen lot o' stuff on his own. So, we'll sort him out first."

"I agree," agreed Charlie. "Let's see how he reacts to the present situation, love." And shoots Evie a warning stare.

"So," asks Constable Waterstone asks the pair. "Was there anything else ya found that ya ain't shared with me yet?"

"We have the size of the shoes that made the tracks." Charlie tells Waterstone. "They were my spread-hand and two of Evie's fingers from heel to toe."

"Well, get a piece of parchment, and put that length on it," the constable instructs. Evie gets up, letting the tea towel fall to the floor and walks to the sink. "Second drawer to the left of the sink, love." Charlie tells her. "Should be a quill and inkwell in there as well, darlin'."

Sure enough, they are indeed there, so Evie takes them out of the drawer and brings them to the kitchen table. Charlie walks over, spreads his right hand on the parchment, and makes a mark where his little finger is. Evie puts her two fingers next to his thumb just like at the print under Betsy and he puts a mark just after her second finger.

"There ya are, constable," Evie tells him, handing him the parchment.

"Thank you, Evie. Do you have a measuring bar, Charlie?" Waterstone asks.

"No, I haven't had a need for one before this, Brien," Charlie tells him.

"That's ok," says the constable. "I have one at me house. Thought I'd use it fer something. Now I know what. So, what you lot got planned fer the night, as if I didn't know."

"Well, yeah, of course," Evie says. "But after that we figger that we'd go back and see if there's anything else ta find, if that's ok. Figure if it rains again, everything'll be washed away, yeah?" She sits back down on the chair, again with her feet on the chair seat, knees covering her naked breasts, not bothering to pick up the tea towel any more.

"I agree." The constable tells them. "the quicker the better, and it being so late, you would have a better chance of seein' somethnig than me, even with tha best torch. Just lemme know what ya find, all right."

"Of course, constable," Charlie assures him. "We'll definitely tell you everything tomorrow. Is Betsy's body at Boyle's as well?"

"Yes, she's lyin' on tha same table as poor Nancy was." Constable Waterstone tells them. "'Course, Nancy's been buried in the pauper's grave already, she were startin' ta stink and Boyle wanted her moved. But we still got both o' their clothes that we can examine."

"Speaking of clothes, love, we might want to put something on before we go out." Charlie says to Evie.

"Oh, all right, love, if you insist." Evie replies. "I s'pose I will… after time." and she smiles in a wickedly sexy way, as she puts her feet on the ground and opens her legs. "Course, we have ta take care o' something before we leave, don't we, love, and we don't have ta get dressed for that, do we?"

"Well, on that note," says the constable. "I'd better get on back home and have me own time with my Flo." And he turns to go, putting on his tricorner.

"Tarrah, then, you two." He says. "Cheers for ya agreein' ta do this." And shakes Charlie's hand. Immediately, Charlie pulls his hand away, searing in pain.

"You all right, mate?" the constable asks.

"I don't know." Charlie tells him, looking down at his palm. The bottom edge of his palm has a deep burn, which quickly disappears. "What happened there?" he asks and looks first to Constable Waterstone, and then to Evie.

"Oh, yeah," she replies without being asked, "my gran'mum also told me that vampyres, well, us, isn't it, we can't touch silver. It burns tha skin, too."

"Oh, it's me ring!" Waterstone says. "Flo give it me for my birthday last month. She always asks me ta wear it and tonight, I decided ta quieten her up and wear it. Sorry, mate didn't know."

"Me either," says Charlie, "thank you so very much for letting me know, Evie." And shoots her a glare.

"Can't think of anything." She tells him, still erotically posed on the kitchen chair. "But I'm sure there'll be something else I ain't thinkin' of just now." And moves her knees back and forth on the chair, aimlessly.

"All right then, you two, cheers, then." Says the constable. "I ain't gonna try that again, so I'll just be on my way."

"Bye then, love." Evie calls as he goes out the door, waving to her.

As soon as the door closes, Evie growls, looks at Charlie through hooded eyes and leaps onto him again. They kiss passionately as she digs her nails into his back through his shirt and waistcoat. His head goes back and his fangs instantly come out and he snarls back at her. He pulls the waistcoat and shirt in one move as the ties and buttons break and the clothes rip in half. He kicks off his shoes as Evie pulls at his groin through his trousers. In one movement, she pulls down his trousers ans tugs his stockings off. Then, as she's already down in front of him, takes his erection into her mouth. Sucking and sucking on him until he pulls her up by her hair and plants her on the table. She wraps her legs around his waist, grasps his erection and pulls him fully inside her. She growls loudly as he fills her vulva. Again and again he pounds into her. Together, they snarl, growl and howl in delight at each other. He lifts her and they continue with her entwined on him as he stands on the floor. He gently sits down on the floor with Evie still on top of him, now. He grabs her by the hips and makes her move with him. Each time they move, she moans in delight and he lets out groans of passion.

Chapter 16

THE SCIENTIST ARRIVES

It takes a full fourty-five minutes for the couple to be completely satisfied with several orgasms each. They drain the last blood-pot, panting, each taking half, get dressed, finally, and head off to Boyle's Butchers again.

As before, the vampyric couple move around back of the butcher's and Charlie finds the key to unbolt the door and move inside, where, as with poor Nancy, Betsy corpse is lying under a bloody sheet on one of the butcher table. In the dark back room, Charlie and Evie survey the scene and remove the sheet from the body. Unilke before, Betsy's clothes are still on. They are as rain-soaked and bloody as they were in the alleyway. The gaping wound on her neck has stopped bleeding and it is clear that the missing front of her larynx is identical to Nancy's injuries.

"Did ya see that?" Evie asks Charlie and points to one of her aqua coloured, crop-sleeved shirt. Of course, Charlie had seen it too, some specks of white powder stuck in the folds of the blouse. "More flour, eh? And this?

"Yeah, and on 'er skirt, ya seen more of them hairs, eh, love?" says Charlie in his common dialect. "And look at 'er fingers." There was dirt, probably from the alley and skin, again, probably scraped from the killer.

It is clear that after the extensive sex they have just had, they are famished again, dspite having half a pot each, that by no means eased their condition. Looking around, Evie spots some parchment paper, lying upon the back counter. She quickly and quietly glides over to the counter and eagerly unwraps the paper. There inside are some hearts and livers from the fresh kills of the day. Charlie joins her and they share the surprise gift they have found.

"We had better give Boyle something for these, then, Evie." Charlie says. "Afer all, he would have got something for them if he sold them, or even made into a pie."

"Sounds only fair ta me, love." she confirms.

He reaches into his purse and removes a one-pound and four shilling coins and puts them on the counter on the unwrapped paper.

"Let's wait and see what the scientist says tomorrow about all this." Charlie says.

"Maybe he's got some of that new equipment, like a micro-glass I've heard about to see tiny things clearer."

"Krikey," Evie comes back with. "Maybe he can even tell exactly about us! And then we'd be in a fine mess, now wouldn't we."

"I'm hoping that Constable Waterstone can sort him out, in that case." He tells her. "He seems to be on our side in all of this."

"Mid-night and all is well!" says the Town Cryer

"I s'pose so," Evie quips back quietly, covering up the body again with the bloody sheet.

"Let's take this pot for the morning, love." Charlie says and takes the one pot on the shelf with him as the pair leave the butcher's shop.

"And I s'pose *I've* gotta carry it again." Evie retorts as she jumps on the horse's back.

"No, love, I thought I might put it on the back this time" he replies, smiling and places the covered blood-pot in one of the rear carriers.

Charlie lights upon Chauncy and they head off to his cottage. On the way, they pass Watchman Masterson carrying his lantern.

"Ayup, you two." He says loudly as they approach. "Off home now, yeah?"

"That's right, Bill." Charlie answers.

"It were nice of the constable ta ask you lot ta help us with tha murders." Waterstone says. "Though I dunno what you could see that none of us could. But I guess more eyes couldn't hurt. Oh, say, ya ain't seen me purse. I lost it somewhere on me rounds earlier."

I saw an empty one outside of The Flying Horse." Charlie tells him. "We've just come from there and if you hurry, it might still be there."

"Oh, bollocks!" Masterson swore. "musta dropped it after havin' a pint" and he winks "or two. Can't wait ta see that scientist in tha mornin'."

"We was hopin' ta meet him as well... at some point." Evie chimes in. "But I wanna take our Charlie here home and shag him proper." And laughs sweetly.

"Well, love, don't let me hold ya, then." The watchman tells her, laughing. "Tarrah, you two."

"Bye," says Charlie and turns Chauncy toward home again.

"Tarrah, Billy," calls Evie as they ride on.

After pulling a rousing session at home, where the slats on the bed are put to a real test... again, Charlie and Evie, each of them are clawed and scratched and bitten severely, collapse into their dead sleep.

The next noon-time weather is delightful, for most people, bright sunshine, the temperatures in the high twenty degrees and low humidity. But for Charlie and Evie, it's disastrous. They can't go out and have no way of sending word to have anyone come to the cottage.

In the meantime, Professor MacWilliams has arrived from London by carriage. He has brought three cases with him, a smaller one has his clothing and the other two larger ones contain various equipment, scales, and manuals to assist him in his work. He is a man of medium height, five feet, eight inches and average weight, 12 stone, a mostly bald head with bushy hair around his ears and back of the head, covered with the typical white wig on top. There are food crumbs spotted in his full, grey beard and half-moon glasses sat low on his nose.

He cordially greets Constable Waterstone at the carriage station near The Flying Horse.

"Ayup, professor," says the constable, extending his hand, which the professor shakes. "May I suggest Tha White Star Inn for your stay, sir?"

"That sounds satisfactory, so long as the room is large enough for my equipment." The professor declares. "I will need to document my findings here for publication."

"I'm sure they have a room large enough to satisfy you' needs." Waterstone replies. "This is gonna be fun." He thinks to himself, sarcastically.

"Let me put my things away and then we can go see the body." He says. "Is there only one?"

"Actually there were two, but we buried tha first one, professor" says the constable. "May I help you with them cases?"

"Yes, thank you, constable." replies the professor and picks up the smallest of the cases, presumably the one with his attire for the next few days and leaves the two larger ones for the larger constable.

They enter The White Star Inn, located on the north side of High Pavement just west of The Flying Horse pub. The professor enters and steps up to the bar area where the barmaid, Janie Winters, greets him.

"Ayup, sirry." She says and looking past the new customer she sees Constable Waterstone struggling behind him with two large cases in hand. "Oh, you must be tha professor everyone's all het up about. I'm Janie" she says.

"Yes, I am Professor MacWilliams and I am in need of premises for a few days stay, my dear." he tells her.

"Fine, I'll get Davy, he's tha manager," she explains. "Can I get ya a drink whilst ya wait?"

"Just a cuppa, please, Janie," he requests. "it's been a long journey from London and that would be nice. Two and milk if you please"

"Of course, professor," she says, pouring and preparing the tea according to his request. "and I'll just get Davy for ya." And departs.

Janie and a black haired heavy-set man return.

"So, professor," says the man. "you need a room Janie tells me."

"Yes," he says between sips of tea. "I just need a room with lots of space."

"'Course. I can give ya Room 4, it's just at tha second floor on the right." Davy instructs him, handing him the key to the room.

"Many thanks, my good man." And leaves with his case in hand. "This way, constable." He leads Waterstone up the circular staircase to the second landing, there on the right is a white door with a "4" on it. The professor inserts the key and turns it all the way round until it opens the door. The room has two beds and a small table along with an en-suite which contains a bath tub and sink with a small mirror above. A full-length mirror is at the back of the door to the room.

"Yes, this will do for a few days." Professor MacWilliams says. "Kindly put the cases on one of the beds and I will use the other one for sleep, constable."

Constable Waterstone hoists the two cases across the spare bed and Professor MacWilliams gently puts his own case next to them.

"I will need to see the body at once." He tells the constable. "If that's convenient for you."

"That would be fine, perfessor." The constable replies. "do ya wanna go now?"

"If it's convenient. Lemme just put some vials and some other equipment in my case and we can go."

The professor opens one of the cases and takes out his leather carry bag. Then reaches in further and takes six empty glass vials, a magnifying glass, measureing rod, tweezers, a knife, and a large lump of wax and puts them all in the bag. He closes the bag and follows Constable Waterstone out of the room, the door of which he locks behind them.

They walk the four shops down High Parliament and walk into Boyle's Butchers.

"Ayup, constable." Mr Boyle greets them with. "Who's yer friend, eh?"

"Oliver, this is Professor MacWilliams." The constable explains. "He's just up from London ta see Betsy and maybe give us some idea who killed 'er."

"Well, perfessor, nice ta meet ya." The butcher says and extends his hand nd the professor shakes it. "Come on in, then. She's just here, and constable, I want 'er out o' here soon as poss, yeah?" And he leads them to the back toom through the curtain.

"Of course," Waterstone states following Boyle. "Soon as we're done here, you can send her ta the cathedral for their sayings and then they'll bury her proper."

They arrive at Betsy's covered body, which the butcher removes, exposing the clothed corpse.

"Anything I can get ya?" the constable asks the professor.

"No, thank you, constable," Professor MacWilliams replies. "but Mr. Boyle, I could use a nice cuppa if you don't mind. Two and milk, please."

"'Course, perfessor." Mr. Boyle says and leaves to get him a cup of tea.

The constable retreats out of the way as the professor starts to his work. He takes out the magnifying glass and looks at the wound first. He takes the measureing rod out of the case and makes several measurements. He then removes a vial form the case and puts some of the skin and blood from the wound into it. Then, he takes the wax out and with the knife cuts off a piece, rolls it in his hands and foms a stopper which he puts in the vial. Mr Boyle returns with the cup of tea and leaves it on the table next to Betsy. The professor drinks some and then continues with his work. He surveys the body from head to toe and discovers the bits of white powder that Charlie and Evie had seen hidden in the folds of her dress. He removes the tweezers and another vial from the case, puts the bits in it with the tweezrs and puts another bit of wax to secure it. He also finds the hairs and puts them into a third wax-stoppered vial.

"This doesn't look like a person's hair," the professor explains to the constable. "Also, this looks like flour, but it could be icing sugar. But I'll know better when I look at it under the micro-scope." putting the sealed vials into the case, shutting it and finishing his tea.

"Many thanks, Mr. Boyle," Professor MacWilliams says to the butcher, and replaces the cup on the table again.

"No worries," says the butcher. Anything I can do ta help." And escorts the two gents out of the front of his shop again. "Well, if ya excuse me. I've got some customers." He shakes both of their hands and heads back behind the counter to wait on Jenna Whealan from The Flying Horse as they walk back to the White Star Inn and the professor's scientific equipment.

"This is going to take me some time, constable," Professor MacWilliams, "so if you've got other work to do, it's going to be pretty boring for you." And he removes the three sealed vials from his bag and some parchment and a lead pencil from the other case.

"Thank you, perfessor," says the constable, "I think I will make my rounds. Would you like to join me for tea later?"

"That would be very nice," Professor MacWilliams tells him absentmindedly, "I will be in need of nourishment by the time I finish my examination. Call on me in an hour, no earlier, to be sure."

"Fine, my good sir," Waterstone says, and holds his hand out for the professor to shake, but he's well into his thought by now. So the constable simply shrugs and heads out of the door.

Chapter 17

SCIENTIFIC DISCOVERY

"Seven o' tha clock and all is well." says the Town Cryer.

Constable Waterstone returns to Professor MacWilliams' room after two hours of making his rounds. As usual, there is nothing amiss in the city. Just the typical goings on of the day: food and wares carts around the green, ladies doing their regular shopping on High Parliament, and the customary street-walking girls dotting most every street around. The constable stops and chats with everyone he encounters, thereby enhancing his reputation of a respected city servant. But now, he must entertain his celebrated visitor and to find out what he's discovered with his sophisticated equipment.

The constable knocks at the door and "Yes, yes," is the response and Professor MacWilliams opens the door. "Come in, constable." he says.

Waterstone enters and sees that on the bed where the cases had been are strewn vials, pieces of parchment with scribbling upon them, the micro-scope and slides, and other equipment of all sorts.

"So, perfessor," asks Constable Waterstone, "have ya found anything?"

"Indeed I have, constable," he starts to answer, when the constable interrupts him.

"Let's chat on our way to tea, then." He says.

"That's a good idea, constable," the professor replies as he puts his wig, tricorner and coat on. "I am getting a bit peckish, my fine fellow." Together they head down the stairs and out the door of the inn as they head down the road.

"I have found that the powder we discovered was indeed icing sugar," the professor begins, "the hairs are from a hare not a person, and the murder weapon is not from a mouth, but from a metal clamp of some sort."

"Owing that the hairs were from a hare and that a metal clamp was involved, makes it seem to me like the weapon might have been some type of animal trap." The constable concludes. "Oh, here we are, The Flying Horse, professor, Jenna has the best food around and the ale is always good." And he opens the door for the guest to enter first.

"'Ayup, Brien," calls Mikey from behind the bar. It is busy as usual, with tables and benches full of regulars home from work, diners, and working girls.

Ayup, Mikey, you all right?" greets the constable.

"Is this that perfessor, then, mate?" he asks. "I think Jenna seen him at Boyle's this afternoon, yeah?"

"Yes, that's right, Mikey," the constable told him. "This is Professor MacWilliams. Professor, this is Mikey. He runs a proper pub here."

"Hello Mikey," says the professor. "We were wondering what you have for tea? Have you a menu?"

"'Course, perfessor," says Mikey proudly. "It's on tha wall just there." And points to the chalk-written items written down. Can I get you two a drink ta start?"

"I'll have a bitter, please, Mikey," says the constable.

"I suppose I'll have the same." The professor adds.

"Order what ya want perfessor," Waterstone says to MacWilliams as Mikey gets their drinks. "I think I'm gonna have tha lamb chops. Is it fresh lamb, Mikey?"

"Just in today from Boyle's," clucked the barman, delivering their beer, "and me Jenna makes her own mint sauce! Her secret ingredient is a pinch a icing sugar." The two men look knowingly at each other.

"Sounds lovely, mate," says the constable slowly. "What ya havin', perfessor."

"I think I'll have the roast beef," the professor declares. "As long as I can have some horseradish with it."

"Janna grows tha horseradish right in tha back o' tha pub!" Charlie tells him. "Onion or brown gravy?"

"Onion, I believe," states Professor MacWilliams, "I don't have to kiss anyone any time soon."

"Ya migh', love, if ya get lucky," says a chubby girl in a bright red dress, who had sidled up next to the visitor as Mikey goes to the back to tell his wife of their selections.

"Thank you, young lady," says the professor. "But, I don't think so. I have a lot of work still to do, and have to document everything, so I need to keep my wits about me. But again, thank you."

"It's ok, sweetheart," says the young girl. "If ya change you mind just ass for Annie, that's me."

"I will, Annie." Professor MacWilliams tells her.

"They botherin' you, perfessor?" asks Jenna with Mikey in tow, looking scandalously at Annie who dances away. "I wish you would sort them out proper," she says as he goes to attend customers at the other end of the bar.

"Oh, no, my dear, it's all right" says the professor, "they're all over, especially in London. In fact you can't walk three lampposts without passing an entire cadre of these ladies there."

"Well, you just let me know and I'll run 'em off, my good sir," she says, "Lemme see how yer tea is gettin' on, gents." And she leaves to go to the back room to inspect their meals.

Mikey returns to them after Jenna has gone. "She get's a li'l het up." He tells them. "Don't know why, they're just tryin' ta make a livin' tha best way they can."

"I know," says Constable Waterstone, "I don't blame 'em for not wantin' ta work in the fields or mills. And if they get a bloke ta marry 'em, then they're out o' that life fer good."

"That's true enough," says the professor.

The two men have another gulp of beer, when Jenna appears again with plates in each hand covered by an oven glove and places them in front of their respective diners, awaiting their opinion. The two men eat the first bite of their dinners and nod appreciatively. Smiling, Jenna again walks through the curtain to the back room.

After another pint each with which to finish their meal, the two gents thank Mikey, the constable pays for their entertainment and they depart the pub.

"What do you think?" asks the professor once they are outside.

"I don't know," answers the constable. "I've known Jenna most of my life. I know she's had a hard time with tha girls'."

"Yes," agrees the professor, "what is that all about?"

"She got together with Mikey later than 'er sisters got married," the constable explains, "and she's afraid that he'll go off with one o' tha girls, I s'pose."

"Anyone else stand out to you, based on my findings, so far?" the professor continues.

"Well, all the families and single women have icing sugar," Waterstone explains. "And there're lots o' animal traps in town ta keep pests out o' their gardens as well as fer food. So we can tick off some people, but not a whole lot."

"Maybe tomorrow will show us some more clues," says his companion. "It's almost ten o' the clock, and I'd best get back and prepare for my bed time. I turn in earlier than you must, sir."

"That's fine, perfessor," says the constable. "I do have a lot o' work ta do meself." And, as he leaves the professor at the door to The White Star Inn, he thinks of Charlie and Evie, and how he can't wait to tell them what the professor has discovered. "Ya know, perfessor, thee's some folk in town I want ya ta meet. They got what ya would call 'special abilities' and I think they might be able ta help us in findin' who done these."

"I look forward to meeting them," the professor says. "Cheers, constable," and he shuts the door to his room. The constable descends the staircase to the pub, says his good-byes to Davy and Evie and heads home.

Chapter 18

HEADS TOGETHER

It's shortly after this that Evie awakes from her repose before Charlie does. She turns to see him with his arms crossed over his heart. She decides that she wants to have a little "fun". Beginning at his toes, she kisses him on her way up her body: his calves, and Charlie stirs; his knees, and he shifts positon; his thighs, and he moans slightly; and pauses to spend time on his manhood, at which he takes her head and ploaces it behind her head, snarling his pleasure. She takes him again into her mouth as his dyorgan grows larger still. He grasps her body and lays it upoon his own so that her groin is just at his mouth and his is at hers. They eagerly suck, lick and probe each others bodies with their mouths and tongues. Charlie then wraps his arms around her waist and stands straight-legged, holding her inverted and continuing their oral gratifications. After much manipulations, they fall on the bed and orgasm together, then Evie swivels her body around, reaches down and inserts Charlie into her quivering vagina. They thrash each other, first on and then off the bed, in their passionate thrawl, as the kitchen table gets knocked over and its content spilled all over the floor and upon the couple, who carry on with their unquenchable desire for each other.

Once they have finished, they dress quickly and head to the stables. The hurriedly attach Chauncy to the carriage, climb aboard and pull their hoods down over their faces. As they ride along Stoney Street onto High Pavement, they are grateful that it's dark as they can barely see through the red haze that tints their vision thoroughly. Likewise, their mouths do not close due to the elongated canine teeth. The couple finally tie the horse up behind The Flying Horse and enter the pub.

"Ayup, ya two," says Jenna to the pair, handing them each a blood-pot. The vampyres remove the covers and quickly drain the contents of the pot. Their teeth return to normal lengths and their vision clears.

"Better now?" Jenna asks, her apron filled with flour, bits of skin, blood and lard, as usual.

"Yes, much," says Charlie as he takes up a second pot. "This should suffice for now."

Evie and Charlie drain the second blood-pot and are feeling like "normal" humans. They thank Jenna for her hospitality and head for the front of the pub, with her trailing behind. They just move through the curtain separating the two parts of the bar, when Constable Waterstone comes through the door.

"Charlie, Evie, it's nice ta see ya, got lots ta tell ya," the constable says. "That professor arrived today and just like you two, he looked at poor Betsy lying in Boyle's and he came up with something." And he tells the pair of the findings from the professor and his equipment.

"Well, that's certainly interesting," says Charlie.

"Yeah," chimes in Evie, "I were sure it was a werewolf who done 'em in."

"Guess you were wrong this time, love," says the constable. "But, you still had tha right idea and seen bowth bodies was killed tha same way. So it figures it was tha same one that done 'em bowth. I might say, don't let on that it ain't a werewolf what done 'em in. This way, whoever *has* done it, will think we're on the wrong track."

"No worries, constable," says Evie, "you can count on me ta keep me mouth shut."

"That would be a first," jokes Charlie." Any idea who that trap might belong to? It's not like people go walking around with animal traps under their arms, is it?"

"No, but if they had a carriage like you lot, then it might be brought along in that." Theorised the constable. "That way, it'd always be handy for 'em, so to speak."

"I see your point," Charlie replies.

"An easy way ta off someone," inserts Evie. "So now all we gotta do is see who's a baker that loves rabbit stew!" and she looks directly at Jenna, cleaning up the tables of plates, cuttlery and glasses. "After all, it *is* one o' her specialities!"

"I know, you're right, Evie," the constable says. "And she definitely don't like your kind millin' about... well, your former kind should I say."

"It's just so, constable," stated Evie matter-of-factly. "She's so jealous of her Mikey that any o' tha girls even sniffs around him, and they practically get a clap round the ear-hole."

"That's true, Evie," Charlie concurs, "but she's not the only one got something against working girls. Not many round here, mind you, but some. Mostly older people or women. Constable, since the trap was probably for rabbits, then even a woman could load and wield it, yeah?"

"I would certainly think so," Waterstone agreed. "So, we've got a carriage with some small rabbit traps in the back and a woman or man carrying them an' killin' tarts. But why rip their throats out and not just stab 'em or something?"

"Guess we'll find out when we catch 'em." Charlie surmised.

"Maybe ta just put us off." suggests Evie. "It certainly did me."

"And why just kill tarts?" asks the constable.

"You know there are still some folks set in the old ways," states Charlie. "Especially older ones or tha ones with firm parents."

"Look, you two, it's gettin' late, an' I gotta get home to Flo," the constable explains. "She worries about me, ya know." and rolls his eyes.

"Of course, Brien," says Charlie, "maybe tomorrow will be rainy and we can come out during the day. That way we can confer with the professor. I would like to share ideas, mate."

"That would be great, Charlie," agrees Waterstone, "I wanna put you lot together, two heads and all."

"Meanwhile, Brien," continues Charlie. "we'll have a look around and see if we can find an unused carriage that's jus' looking for a hare trap to travel with."

They say their "tarrah's" to each other, and the constable heads on back to his house, and Charlie and Evie re-enter the pub.

"So, have ya met tha perfessor, yeh?" asks Mikey as he sees them. "Seems a nice bloke, him."

"No, maybe tomorrow, Mikey," replies Evie. "'Course it'll have ta be rainin' fer us ta go out in tha daytime."

"So, ya need some more pots, yeah?" Mikey asks. "We only got two from Boyle's, but I hear that Tha White Star, got some fresh liver and kidney from a butcher on tha other side o' town. I already told our Davy there that ya might be stoppin' by to have a taste."

"So, he knows about our condition, then." Asks Charlie.

"No, no," Mikey assures them. "I told him that you had a special recipe for steak and kidney pie that calls for liver as well."

"What a clever boy you are," Evie says. "You deserve a reward." And looks lustily at Mikey.

"Evie, why don't you leave Mikey to Jenna and us to see about that meal from The White Star, eh?" Charlie admonishes her. "Many thanks, Mikey, you've been really helpful with our situation."

"That's right, Mikey," agrees Evie. "Ya sure there's nothin' I can do ta thank you?"

"He's sure, Evie," says an angry Jenna, who suddenly appears, arms folded in front of her. "Now, you can clear out b'fore I accidental-like tip out yer food, so ta say." It seems odd to the pair that Jenna is wearing a long-sleeved shirt during this hot weather, though they say nothing about it.

"We'd best leave, love," Charlie instructs, whispering. Then to Jenna, "may we have the two pots, Jenna, before something really does happen to them?"

"Carry on, then," she replies, arms still folded, glaring at Evie. "You know where they are."

Charlie and Evie move through the curtain, to the back and take the two blood-pots off the shelf and head out the back door to the pub.

"You mind 'er, now Charlie," calls Jenna, who suddenly appears in the back, with unchanged arms, "b'fore someone might rip out her throat!"

"And you might mind yerself," Evie snidely answers, "b'fore I might forget ta feed some night and come lookin' fer a snack, darlin'." And her eyes get angry and her canines start to lengthen.

"Evie," shouts Charlie from outside. "come with me. Now."

"Tarrah, Jenna," Evie sideways, a wicked smile on her lips, as her teeth retract to their regular length. She puts her pot into the carriage next to Charlie's and the two walk around the corner of the pub and head toward The White Star Inn.

"What was *that*?" asks Charlie once they're away from the pub.

"I was just tryin' ta wind 'er up," explains Evie as they walk, "maybe make her bring out her hare trap. I weren't in no trouble, ya know. I can take care o' meself, love."

"Oh I have no doubts my dear." Assures Charlie, and they turn into the front of The White Star pub.

Chapter 19

WHAT, ANOTHER ONE?

"Ayup, me ducks," calls Janie, the barmaid, cheerfully, "What can I get ya?" The pub is not nearly as busy as The Flying Horse, but there are still some dining customers at tables and working girls milling around.

"Ayup, Janie," says Charlie. "understand that Mikey from The Horse called on ya, saying that we'd be by for some heart and kidney."

"Oh, you're tha ones, are ya?" asks Janie. "It's nice ta see ya again, Evie. Been a while, love."

"Nice ta see you, too, Janie," replies Evie. "How ya goin' on, then?"

"We' been fine, me an' Davy," says Janie, "you?"

"Well, I guess ya could say I been through some changes of station," says Evie, "me and my Charlie, see, we don't like tha daylight, if ya take my meanin'. But, whilst we get up, or b'fore we go ta sleep, that's when we get ta havin' a bit o' fun together." And laughs knowingly.

"Well, then, dearie," Janie says. "good fer you, good fer you. Ya got yerself a keeper there, Charlie dear. Now let's see about them innards for ya, yeah?" and she leads Charlie to the back room through the curtain behind the bar.

"I'll be back in two ticks, love," he says to Evie, "try not to get into trouble, eh?"

"Evie?" says a voice from behind her. "Evie, is that you? Ya look so different, all pale-like."

Evie turns to see who's speaking, "Susie, how good ta see ya me ducks." She says. "How ya goin' on then, love?" Susie is pleasant-looking, but not as striking as Evie, with dirty blonde hair cut into a fringe in front and long at the back. She's dressed in a pink puffy-sleeved dress and although she's short and slightly stocky, she fills in the dress most alluringly. Her smile makes Evie, and I'm sure her customers as well, feel at ease.

"Oh, ya know, all right, I s'pose," Susie replies, suddenly looking down sadly. "It ain't tha same round tha flat, Nancy was really nice and kind, ya know, it's a horrible thing, ain't it? I been callin' her name lots o' times an' theres no one there."

"Yeah, it is, Susie," Evie says. "That's why Charlie 'n me are helpin' tha constable in lookin' into who done it."

"You two?" asks Susie, "oh, wait you're an Observant ain't ya. I forgot, what with all o' this goin' on."

"Yes, and so is our Charlie," added Evie. "Now."

Right on cue, Charlie returns with Janie trailing behind, carrying several paper wrapped bundles in his arms.

"We can add these to the pots at The Horse, dear," he says to her. "This should keep us for a few days, yeah?"

"Yeah, it should at that, love," she agrees. "Well, Susie, we're gonna be off now, love. We'll see you again, soon. Be careful o' yerself, yeah?"

"Oh, yeah, love, I will, sweetheart," she answers, "you know how cautious I am."

"I do, love," Evie replies, "that's why I said something, do be careful, somone is killin' girls and I don't want ya ta be next."

"Thanks, Evie," Susie says, "I'll be seein' ya, love."

They leave the pub and head down the street, again finding their empty carriage waiting behind The Flying Horse. They place the wrapped organ meat alongside the blood-pots in the back. Then they climb aboard and head off down High Pavement in the opposite direction from Charlie's house.

"You know, love," Charlie starts as they ride along, "I have concluded that the reason no one has heard either Nancy or Betsy cry out is that they were comfortable with their attacker and by the time they realised they were in trouble, they had their throats ripped out, so they couldn't do."

"That makes sence, love," Evie agrees. "so all we gotta do is see who can come up on someone without girls bein' scared, especially now. And if they trusted that person, that wouldn't put 'em off, yeah?"

"Of course," he says, "and this is what I can't suss out."

"When you do, love, you'll let me know, yeah?" she teases him.

"One o' tha clock an all is well," calls the Town Cryer.

"Well, Evie," says Charlie, "there are four stables with carriages that we can look at."

"And don' ferget," she reminds him, "some got their own carriages, as well, like Jenna an' Mikey."

"That's true, but let's look at the ones that we know about first." He says.

They ride on High Pavement and turn onto Castle Gate where Loggin's Stables is located. Many of the upper class townspeople keep their rides here, owing to its location near The Castle. Certainly, the types of carriages are not the typically plain ones, used by most of the rest of Nottingham. It would certainly be a surprise to see someone of good standing involved in such a terrible set of occurances, Charlie surmises, and that they leave no stone unturned. But, as constable Waterstone told them, it could be anyone.

They disembark from their own carriage and look at the first of three roofed, ornate ones parked outside the stables. It's a deep red colour with golden with scrollwork adorning the sides. The front bars, holding the two required horses in place, made of elegant mahogany. The windows of the carriage are decorated with pink linen drapes. Charlie and Evie open the doors on each side and peer inside. Even in the pitch darkness, they can see that there is no hair nor indentation on the claret coloured felt carpeting on the floor from traps and smell that there is no blood present. They inspect the other two carriages, a royal blue one with pale yellow curtains and deep yellow carpetting and a black one with light greay curtains and carpetting. In each case, there are no tell-tale signs of foul play that they can detect. The interior of each one is in the same spotless condition that are required by the customers that Loggin provides for.

"Well, love," says Evie, "Nothin here, then. Where we off to next?"

"I figure Walkers' Stables on Friar's Lane, just ahead." He tells her, as they climb aboard their carriage and nudge Chauncy into motion. It takes less than five minutes to get to the next stable where carriages are kept. The two people carriers are much less decorated than the last lot they inspected, but still have roofs and the windows just move up and down in place. The carriages themselves are plain black with no scrollwork adorning the sides, and the rails connecting it to the two-team horses are polished oakwood. Charlie and Evie get down off their ride and open the doors on each side of the first carriage. The floor is plain wood, so there would be no indentations from the traps, if there were any contained there, but there is plenty of dirt on it as, clearly, Mr. Walker is not the tidiest of people. Even in the dirt, there are no impressions from whatever might have been there, just muddled footprints. Additionally, here again, no hairs are seen and no blood is smelt. The identical situation exists as the second and third identical carriages are investigated by the pair. The carriages here and at Loggin's are both much larger than Charlie's open one that Chauncy can handle on his own.

You know, Evie," begins Charlie, "at least two people would have to load, drive and put away the horses and carriage, which seems unlikely to have happened, owing to the circumstances of two murders taking place."

"I see what ya mean," Evie replies, "so, we gotta find a place what has smaller carriages."

"I was just thinking about that," answers Charlie, "and that's our next stop."

At that, Charlie and Evie climb back into their carriage, give Chauncy a light clap of the reigns, and head off to their next destination: Vandy's Stables on Angel Row. Charlie knows that they have some, more common, carriages capable of being handled by one person which would be required to commit these crimes. Continuing on Friar's Lane, they turn left onto Beast Hill which becomes Angel Row, they turn into the long drive to the stables and, parked round the side, they find three plain, open-aire carriages and they both notice wheel marks and hoof prints from where a fourth one must have been kept, but is curretly being used just now. As they look at the first one, there's mud on the floor upon which are more muddled footprints, but no hairs and they smell no blood. The second one is in a similar condition, but in the back of the third one, there are some hairs, which Charlie puts in his pouch and blood splashes that they smell, even though it is a faint odour.

"I think we gotta find who's used this carriage, then, yeah?" Evie says.

"But, if they just took the carriage that was used for the killings before that, then there'd be no way of knowing who it was, is there?" asks Charlie, "And that's what we need to know if we're gonna collect that reward."

"So, what we gonna do, then, love?" asks Evie.

"We can tell the constable what we've found," Says Charlie, "and let him ask Mr. Vandy who it was that has taken this carriage. But we have to be careful not to accuse just anyone, killing someone is a terrible crime, it leads to either banishment to America or..."

Just then another police whistle blow is heard, interrupting Charlie.

"C'mon, love, we better see what's goin' on," Evie says and the two vampyres climb back up into the carriage, turn it around and give Chauncy a firm clap from the reigns this time, and head back down Angel Row toward the sound of the watchman's whistle blows.

They continue on as the names of the road continually change: from Angel Row to Beast Hill, to Wheeler Gate, and, just past the Market Place, to Pepper Place. They then turn left on Bridle Smith Gate, always following the sound of the whistle. As the look ahead of them, about 30 metres down Bridle Smith, they see Watchman Masterson blowing his whistle anxiously. He's stood in front of another alleyway between buildings looking around as he keeps blowing intermittently.

"Well, seems you two are always around when we need a hand." says the watchman. "and Constable Waterstone likes havin' you around as well."

"What's the trouble, Watchman?" asks Charlie to Masterson, who puffs up his chest when Charlie refers to him by his official title.

"We got another one, mate." Says the official. "Another tart got herself killed. Throat torn out just like tha other ones. Why don't tha two o' you see what you can see there?"

"You know who it is, Billy?" asks Evie.

"Yeah, it's Susie," he tells her. "She works at..."

Evie rushes into the alley to see the dead corpse of the girl that she just spoke with in The White Star a short space of time ago. There's a blood pool around her neck wound and staining her pink dress and her eyes are still open, with a blank stare in them. The sight of it fills Evie with mixed feelings: sorrow for the girl she knew who was so brutally killed, and excitement at seeing all that lovely fresh human blood! She bends down and sucks some of the blood off of the dress and then off of the ground.

Charlie walks down the alley slower, following Evie, then, seeing the blood-soaked body and Evie's drenched face, says to the constable without looking at him, "I think we've got everything sorted here, Bill, you go on back 'n' keep sight on tha front, ok?" he can feel his own blood rising at the sight. He then bends down over where Evie drinking, covering her body with his own and closes Susie's eyes.

"That's a good idea, Charlie," Watchman Masterson says as he trails behind the pair but then turns around again, "I'll let ya get ta yer work, then." He calls over his shoulder. He moves to the front of the alley again, where he continues blowing his whistle, officially.

Meanwhile, Charlie bends over and joins Evie as they enjoy the first taste of human blood in a good long while. They peruse the scene carefully and notice dirt and skin under Susie's fingernails, and white powder on her dress, just the same as with both Nancy and Betsy. They wipe their mouths with Susie's dress and then head back up to the front of the alleyway.

"Must've just happened," the watchman tells them, shaking his head, "I heard a horse's whinny, a crack of a whip, and a carriage's wheels take off quick-like. With all tha trouble we've been havin' I thought I'd have a look, and I come across 'er lyin' there. She was still alive when I come, but couldn't say nothin'. I even asked!"

"I'm sure you did, Watchman," says Charlie. "Did she in any way indicate who her attacker was, then?"

"I'm sorry, Charlie," the watchman told them, "she was just fightin' for her life, mate. And then she up and died just where she was."

"Yes, I see that, Bill," Charlie tells him. "What do you make of the skin under her fingernails, then, mate?"

"Skin?" the watchman asks, "I didn't see no... skin. Maybe she scratched tha killer or something, or maybe it's just chicken skin," he suggests.

"Chicken skin?" says Evie incredulously, "Susie didn't know how ta cook nothin'. Nancy done all o' their cookin'... when they was alive that is."

"I sent a runner over ta get tha constable." Masterson tells them. "He's gonna be real angry when he gets woke up this time o' night. And Flo is gonna be down-right fumin'."

The all wait at the alley's mouth until, some time later, Constable Waterstone arrives, looking bleary-eyed.

"Well, Bill, what we got, then," asks the constable, "tha kid you sent said that there's a third dead tart. Is that true?"

"'Fraid so, sir," says the watchman, "It's Susie, tha tart from the White Star. You know, Nancy's flatmate."

"What you find?" asks Waterstone of Evie and Charlie.

"Just more 'o tha same," replies Evie, "throat out, powder on 'er dress, skin under 'er nails. Tha usual, I'm afraid."

"I'd check that powder again with your professor," Charlie asks him. "It may be the same, but it may not. We'd be very interested."

"Got it," says the constable. "Are you two gonna meet him tomorrow? It's a cloudy moon tonight, and, according ta me auntie, usually means rain, or at least real overcast, then."

"He's right, love," confirms Evie, "me gran'mum says the same."

"That gran'mum of yours musta been a right-proper gypsy, sweetheart," Charlie tells her, "Well, constable, if it is cloudy tomorrow, then, of course, we'll meet tha professor. What's his name, Brien?"

"Perfessor MacWilliams," says Constable Waterstone. "He's a real smart one, he is. You'd like him now. I put him up in tha big room at tha White Star. He seems comfy there. Got all his stuff on one bed and he's sleepin' in tha other one."

"Do you want us to just go over in the morning, by ourselves, then Brien?" asks Charlie.

"Yeah, that's fine, mate," says the constable, "I'm probably gonna sleep in with all this tonight and I'll meet ya there. Say around... nine? If you can get out. If not, I'll bring tha perfessor to yours around ten."

"We'll see ya tomorrow, then," says Evie as they climb aboard their carriage, "one way or tha other." And they ride off back down the road to Charlie's house.

Chapter 20

MEETING THE PROFESSOR

After putting Chauncy into the stable, and the bridle and carriage away, Charlie and Evie bring the blood-pots and wrapped organ meat into the house and place them on the table. Of course, Evie is feeling a bit randy once they're inside and alone, and she slowly strips off her attire, looks at him seductively through the fringe of her auburn-coloured tresses and sits Charlie down on the bed, then takes a position on his lap with her back to him, bare feet on the floor, gyrating her nude form on his growing organ. He grips her around her waist and digs his nails into her hips. She then stands, lifts him up, strips him off, and repositions herself just above his hips, this time facing him, knees on either side of his hips and her hands on his shoulders. She moves gently as she feels him grow even larger beneath her and not using her hands, moves so that his enlarged organ is now poised at the mouth of her womb. She moves again slightly and takes him inside with a moan on her part and flips her hair as the cranes her neck back in ecstasy. They move together in perfect unison, first slowly and then, very soon, thrashing again with Evie on top, now pushing him down onto the bed with him still inside as she moves up and down, ripping at his chest and he grips her breasts tightly, pulling her down even more forcefully, as they orgasm together and growl loudly as they do so.

Recovering, but not bothering to dress, they sit at the table and share their spoils of the organ meat. At once, their red vision clears and teeth retract. By now, it's almost daybreak and Evie peers carefully outside to see the severly cloudy day with threatening rain; it's the perfect day for a meet and greet if it stays such. Charlie decides that it might be a good idea to dress before going out. So they put on clothes from the wardrobe and throw the items they had been wearing under the bed for taking to the washer woman tomorrow... or the next day. Charlie ties his purse containing the hair from the carriage around his belt. They step out of the house together and glide silently to the barn.

"Ayup, you two," calls a voice from inside which they identify as Mr. Firthe, "didn't hear ya come up. Where ya off to, then?"

"We gonna meet tha perfessor that's visitin' from London Town," explains Evie. "Then, we got some information fer him, and see what we can do ta find out who done them killin's."

"So, workin' with tha constable, then, Evie, yeah," says Mr. Firthe. "You on with that as well, Charlie?"

"I am, Mr. Firthe," Charlie assures him. "Can we help you, then?"

"I just wanna make sure you're ok with my takin' care o' Chauncy, lad," the stableman says, "Oh, an, jus' make sure ya wanna find tha answers, mate. It could be quite a surprise, lad; I mean it could be anybody."

"That's true, you never know, Mr. Firthe," Charlie asserts. "Do you know anything about the murders?"

"Nothin' worth mentioning," he says. "I know just what everyone else does, three tarts got themselves killed and no one knows who done it."

"Anything else?" Charlie asks. "Seems you were hinting that you had some new information."

"Nah," Mr. Firthe replies, "I was just talkin'. I likes ta read lotsa stories on stuff like that, and thought maybe it might be like one o' them books."

"Oh, ok, Mister Firthe," Evie says to him, and shoots Charlie a quick look that she knew that Mr. Firthe wouldn't notice. "sounds all right. Please just let Charlie or me know if'n ya think o' something that might help, love, yeah?"

"O' course, darlin'," says Mr. Firthe. "If'n I find anything, you lot will be tha first ta know. Charlie, ya gonna need tha carriage, again, today?"

"Yes, if it stays like this, we're going to have to be careful of the rain," At that, Charlie and Mr. Firthe remove Chauncy from his stall and bring him round to where the carriage is kept. The hook him to it and Charlie and Evie climb aboard, silently.

"Good luck you two," calls Mr Firthe and heads inside the barn again.

Charlie and Evie head down Stone Street and turn back again onto High Pavement until they arrive at The White Star Inn. It's half-eight as they tie Chauncy up at the railing of the pub and step inside.

"Ayup, Charlie. Evie," calls Janie from behind the bar, her eyes are red, and they can tell she's been shedding tears. "It's horrible what's happened ta poor Susie 'n' tha others." She blubbers and starts to cry again into her apron. "She were here just b'fore she got killed. I feel so baaaad."

"It's not your fault, Janie," Charlie tells her. "There's nothing you could have done. And you might have been killed right along with her."

"Oooooh", she wails. "Don' even *say* that, Charlie, it does my head in just thinkin' about it."

"I know, Janie," Charlie tells her, "it upsets us all. That's why we're here, love. We're gonna work with the professor to find out who's done it. Which room is he in?"

"Room 4 upstairs and yes, he's there," says Davy coming into the bar from the front room through the door. "Now Janie, dear, you go on and take care of Tommy and Jill at the table. They look very thirsty."

And the teary-eyed barmaid retreats to the other end of the pub where a gent and a working girl are snogging soppily over breakfast. Janie comes up to them and she asks them if they'd like more tea. They come up for air just long enough for him to say, "Yes". She clears the breakfast dishes on the bar and goes to the large tea kettle to fill smaller teapot from it, then returns to the amorous couple. Jill has her hand now discretely at the gent's belt, looking for his purse. Evie watches the scene and moves over to the couple as Janie moves away, where she slaps Jill's hand, "Now, Jill, love, you know that our Tommy here needs all his coins for his poor mum at home, he don't need ya ta borrow those just now."

The girl Jill looks at Evie with a glare that would kill... if she weren't dead already! But she says nothing and resumes snogging with Tommy, who warily, now, continues his affections as well.

Evie goes back to stand with Charlie. "I know he's still up there because 'e ain' been down ta breakfast yet. So you want something?" the barman asks.

"Cheers, Davy," Charlie says, "we've already eaten this morning, mate. Say, what time is he usually up?"

"Well, mate, yesterday it were in about in an hour," Davy said. "Can ya go off and come back, then?"

"I think we can find something to keep us occupied," Charlie says, and winks at Davy. "But, maybe if it's only an hour, a checkers game will suit us just as well."

"Sure enough, mate, got tha pieces just here behind tha bar," Davy tells them, reaching for the game pieces in a small wood box.

He hands them to Charlie, "What's tha winner get, eh, love?" Evie asks as she takes the box from him and walks silently over to the checker table and sits straddling the low stool.

"Guess we'll have to come up with something, yeah?" says Charlie, "How about the winner doing whatever he" "Or she" Evie interrupts, "or she," he continues, "wants the other to do when we get back home."

"*That* sounds terribly naughty, sweetheart," Evie says still in earshot from Davy, stroking her long hair, legs still splayed apart under her dress. "But, fun, win *or* lose!"

"Should kill some time, eh Charlie?" Davy says to them. And Charlie sits down at the game table across from Evie to start the match. "Can I get ya anything?"

"That's all right, Davy," says Charlie, quickly intent upon the game at hand. "We're alright, thanks."

The game lasts almost the entire hour as they keep watching the doorway, awaiting the arrival of the professor. Charlie jumps the last two of Evie's pieces with his last king and wins the game.

"What ya wanna jump now, love?" she asks him, leaning forward, and grabs her breasts which are nearly exposed from her puffy top.

"That'll have to wait, babe," Charlie tells her, "we have to meet up with this professor."

"S'pose so," she says, leaning back upright, and gives him a wicked little smile.

Just as they are putting the pieces back into the box as Davy rushes up to them, "There he is, you two. Tha Perfessor, in tha brown jacket and waistcoat, with tha tan stockings. I'll send him over, ok?"

"Yes, Davy," Charlie tells him, "I'm looking forward to speaking with him."

The professor is stood at the bar and orders a breakfast with a full pot of tea. "There're some folks that wanna meet ya, perfessor." Davy tells him, pointing to where Charlie and Evie are sat. They wave at him and Charlie waves him over to sit with them. The professor gets his cuppa and brings it over to the gaming table.

"You two must be the ones that Constable Waterstone informed me about." He says as he sits down at the table, Charlie on his left and Evie on his right. "He has told me that you have special skills that will be helpful. I use the scientific method to solve these intricate problems."

"Yes, professor, we do have some... abilities... that we want to combine with your skills to find who has done these killings. But, let's move to a more comfortable table and we'll let you eat first, then we can go to see the equipment you've brought with you. And put together what you've found with what we know." He says.

They move to one of the tables along the wall, Evie and Charlie on one side, Professor McWilliams sat across from them as Janie brings over his breakfast.

"Would you like something yourselves?" he asks.

"Many thanks, professor, but we've already had something earlier," Charlie tells him. "You go on, then."

"Oh my dear, I should have told you I don't like blood pudding." He says to Janie, as she leaves the plate, and turns to go. "Oh well, no matter, I'll just leave it, though I do hate to waste foods." Her shoulders slump at his admonition.

"Give it a go, perfessor," Janie tells him, sadly. "I made it fresh today. It's me own secret recipe."

"Yes, it *is* quite nice, Janie," he tells her. "Is that cinnamon?"

"Well spotted, love," Janie replies proudly, although still sad. "That's my secret ingredient." She then leaves him to his meal, and moves, head still down, back behind the bar.

"So, perfessor," Evie starts to say. But he just holds his index finger in the air to have her hold her enquiry. "I prefer to eat in the quiet." He explains to her as he quickly finishes the rest of his breakfast in silence. They are amazed that someone so slight can put away food that fast.

"Thank you," the professor tells them after eating. "Now, what would you like to do first?" And takes a gulp of tea.

"Let's see what ya found out and then, we tells you what we knows," Evie says, brashly.

"Ah, my dear, an exchange of information, that sounds like a viable plan," Professor McWilliams. "Follow me up to the room, and I'll show you what I have." He finishes his cuppa in one long gulp.

"Many thanks Janie," he calls to the barmaid as they get up to leave. "I'll have to remember to tell my local to put cinnamon in their blood pudding. It truly added something very nice."

She half-smiles back as they leave the bar area and the three of them start to ascend the stairs to the visitor's room.

"Oi, perfessor," Janie glumly calls to him, on the stair. "Can ya tell yer friends in London about me 'n' my recipe?"

"Oh, my dear, I most certainly will." He calls back.

A slight smile moves across her face, much smaller than it normally is.

The trio ascend the two sets of spiral stairs to room 4, where Professor McWilliams unlocks the door and steps back as Charlie and Evie enter the room. There are note-covered-parchment, equipment, and slides strewn across the one bed with the other completely unkempt. In the the door to the wardrobe is ajar, so its contents are completely visible: clothes, gloves and hats are shoved onto the floor of the clothes-container randomely and the professor's case is on top of the wooden structure itself.

"Let me show you what I've discovered, and then I'll hear what you have to say." He says excitedly. He moves over to the scientific bed and picks up a parchment. "You see, I've made notes on what I found. There are bits of animal fur, fats, and blood, along with the victim's blood, of course, in the first wound. But looking at it under my inspecting glass, I could tell there were two distinct *types* of blood."

"Types of blood?" Evie asks. "Ain't all blood tha same?" And she looks at Charlie.

"Well, my dear, whilst the main parts of all blood are identical, there are subtle differences that can only be seen when examined carefully." The professor explains.

"And that white powder. Was it flour, like we thought?" Evie asks.

"Actually, it was icing sugar." The professor tells her. "There was also skin, probably from the killer, under her nails."

"Yes, we noticed and concluded that as well." Charlie tells him.

"So, what information have you for me? Professor McWilliams asks.

"Well, perfessor," Evie begins. "There's been another murder. It's another tart and she use ta work here!"

"Well, that means that there's even more evidence for us to examine, then." The professor says excitedly. "Was there anything else before we leave to look at the scene?"

Charlie unties his purse and opens it, pulling out the tiny hairs he had collected at Vandy's Stable the night before and giving them to the professor.

"Thought you might tell us if these are the same types of hairs as were on the poor dead girls." Charlie says.

"Well, I'll certainly give it my best efforts." He tells them. "Put them here," and takes out a small cutting table from somewhere on the "equipment bed".

Charlie places the small hairs on the table and the professor gently, but quickly, takes them to where the microscope is on the dressing table. He takes the tweezers and places a few of them on a glass slide with a cover slide atop. He then lights the candle under the microscope stand and places the slide with the hairs upon it. He looks through the eyepiece.

"Hmmm," he says. "M-hmm. No, I would say they are not the same types of hairs. Not a human hair, mind you, but, no, not the same as the others."

"I'm sure she is," Charlie replies. "So, professor, any idea what type of hair these might be?"

"Animal, no doubts," he says, looking back through the eyepiece. "Maybe dog... or...

"Is it a wolf's hair, then, perfessor?" Evie asks.

"No, too small and thin to be a wolf or dog." He says, still peering into his microscope. "Where did you find it?"

"At a stable in near here." Evie tells him. "Say, perfessor, how long ya been on yer own, then?"

"What? How did you know, my dear?" he asks her, turning around, stunned.

"Well, yer shirt got stains... mustard, I'd say. Yer stokings got small holes, probably from yer cat. And yer hat is all dusty and not just from tha trip here." She explains.

"Well, I can certainly see why the constable thought you might be valuable in detecting work." He says. "And, yes, my wife has been visiting her family down in Portsmouth, for the last month. She's due home in a fortnight. It'll be good to have a fresh-cooked meal. Not that my local is bad, but my Danielle is a right-good cook, I'll tell ya."

"So, what kind of animal did it come from?" Charlie asks.

"I think it probably is... no wait... bovine! Yes, that's got it!" the professoer explains.

"Sorry, perfessor, what's a bow-vine?" Evie asks.

"Cow, love," Charlie tells her, "it's a *cow's* hair. Right, professor?"

"Absolutely or goat. They're in the same animal family. No doubt." He confirms. "The person who killed this woman had close contact with these animals. Maybe a butcher or a farmer?"

"Gee, we ain't got none o' them around here, have we Charlie." Evie says sarcastically, rolling her eyes, as she brushes her hair over her bare shoulders.

"Aren't sheep of the same family as well?" Charlie asks.

"Indeed they are, but their hair is longer and more, well, 'fleecy'." The professor corrects him. "There were no hairs of that type on this girl's body. And yes, I know dear, there are many of both types of professions around here. So anyone could have done these crimes. It just makes our job that much more difficult, I'm afraid."

"We keep saying and hearing that..." explains Charlie, "now, all we have to do is find the proper needle. But at least we're in the right haystack."

"Indeed, Charlie." states Professor McWilliams. "Shall we go, then?" and he starts to collect his scientific equipment from the bed and put them into his science bag.

"I thought we'd wait until Constable Waterstone gets here," says Charlie.

"Oh, is he meeting us here?" the professor asks.

"That was tha original plan," replies the constable from the door, stopping Professor McWilliams from gathering his things.

"I just said that because I knew you were here, Brien," explains Charlie, gleefully.

"You smelled him too, eh?" Evie whispers to Charlie, smiling. "Nice breakfast, mate." She says to the constable.

"Yeah, my Flo makes a nice one fer me." He replies. "She even makes blood pudding with cinnamon, like Janey downstairs does. But we'd best be off ta see about poor Susie."

"Still cloudy out there, is it?" Evie asks.

"Yes, and it's started raining a bit," answers Constable Waterstone. "So you two can go out with us." And he gives them a knowing look that the professor, who has resumed collecting equipment into his bag, doesn't even acknowledge. He is too busy muttering to himself as he completes his foraging.

Once he has finished packing his bag, the group set off down the stair again, Constable Waterstone leading the way, followed by Professor McWilliams, Evie and Charlie.

"Guess we'll let him go first," Evie whispers to Charlie as they reach the ground floor landing. "After all, we already seen poor Susie."

Chapter 21

CLOSING THE LOOP

They exit the pub and it's still raining and overcast as the quartet walk to the crime scene, where Watchman Masterson is discovered sleeping on the bench at the end of the alley. He apparently has been there all night, "guarding" the crime scene.

"Bill," calls Constable Waterstone as they four of them approach. "Bill, wake up, mate, it's time ta go home, lad."

Drowsily, the watchman stirs, "Constable? Is that you?" the watchman asks. "I'm still on duty, sir. No worries."

"That's fine, Bill, you can go home now," the constable replies. "We're here now, it's all right."

"Thank you, Brien," says Watchman Masterson, "I think I will 'ead on home, now. I think I need some sleep."

Charlie and Evie look at each other through the raindrops and smile, acknowledging the humour of the situation with the poor, exhausted Watchman.

As they enter the alleyway, the overhanging rooftops block the rain from disrupting the evidence. They approach the deceased body of poor Susie. The constable and the professor kneel down to inspect the wound and body.

"See here?" the professor asks. "Here at the edges of the wound on her neck, it looks like there was a first attempt which was too much for the trap to grasp. So they withdrew it and gave it a second go. They must have been very strong in the hands to hold this poor child for so long. And here, under her nails," and holds up her left hand then her right, "skin, again. Whoever has done these crimes, must have terrible scratches on their arms and maybe her face, too"

Charlie and Evie have been standing away from the scene, so as not to get tempted to drink the coagulating blood remaining in Susie's decomposing corpse. But this separation allows them to survey the scene more completely.

"Ge-ents." calls Evie, sing-songy. "Come see what me 'n' Charlie found out here!"

The constable and professor rise and follow the two vampyres to the mouth of the alley. The pair are standing around the bench where the Watchman had been sleeping. He had clearly moved he bench from its normal location to its new position in order to "protect" the murder scene. But clearly, the repositioning of the bench, as well as the sleeping body of the Watchman, had kept whatever had been there intact from the downpouring rain. And with Charlie and Evie being Observants, it was easy for them to see what was obscured underneath the bench itself.

"If ya move that bench, lads," Evie instructs the pair, "you can see what we seen."

The two men move to each end of the bench and lift it away from its position. Clearly, Charlie or Evie could have each easily moved the entire bench by themselves, but they wanted the two others to shift its position to "discover" the hidden secret beneath.

There was a relatively dry "T" on the ground where the bench-feet made an impression and where it was obvious the Watchman slept as well as the large heel impressions perpendicularly about 2 metres away from the bench. Just at the intersection of the "T", there it was. Charlie and Evie had seen it on their first look at the scene last night, but it was a revelation for the two "professionals", a clear hoof-print. But the remarkable thing about this hoof-print was that it wasn't a complete print; there was a clear piece in the corner that was missing from the horseshoe!

"Well, *this* can't be very common", surmises Constable Waterstone. "All we have ta do now is find out who has a horse what's missin' a chunk out of their horseshoe."

"It'd be easier if we had the piece that's missing." says the professor.

"I think Evie and I could do that on our own," Charlie explains. It'll also give them a chance to feed again before their hunger starts to overtake them. Plus, as they get more hungry for blood, their sexual appetite grows as well; not that it isn't usually rampant for each other all the time at any rate, but it is almost insatiable when the hunger gets on them.

As if on cue, Evie tugs at Charlie's sleeve, "After all, I do have to pay you off for losing at rounders, don't I?" she whispers to him, with a lascivious smile on her face. He smiles back down at her.

"You'll let us know if ya find anything, yeah?" calls the constable after them. "We'll stay here and see what we can find."

"Of course, Brien," calls back Charlie.

The professor says to the constable, "Do you know where I can get some paper mache?"

The couple look curiously at each other as they turn the corner and Charlie puts Evie against the brick wall of the building and they kiss passionately. She wraps her left leg around his right one, pulling him tight to her. He can feel her nipples harden beneath her thin top and she can feel his erection growing larger through his trousers. Each of their eyes are fire red and their teeth are completely elongated as well as they entwine their bodies against the wall of the building. Evie's skirt rides up to her waist, exposing her fanny. She takes hold of Charlie's right hand and thrusts it onto her clit as she moans in anticipation of penetration. All of a sudden, a voice calls out from the corner of the building:

"Oi, you two, come away from my shoppe! Take it on home, you lot!" it's Mr. Cinders, the baker. "Charlie? Is that you?"

"Yeah," Charlie responds breathing hard, dipping his head so that the baker can't see his changed visage. "You ok, Mr. Cinders?" And he takes his hand away from Evie's mound.

"Yeah, you?" the baker answers. "Is that Evie with you? Ain't seen her manky fanny round here for a while." And she tosses her hair and peers through her fringe and around Charlie to sneer at Mr. Cinder.

"She's with me, Mr. Cinders!" Charlie tells him defiantly. "Have a care how ya speak to 'er. Or about 'er." And looks him directly in the eye.

"I... I'm sorry, Charlie... Evie," Mr. Cinders says suddenly shrinking back. "Could ya kindly move it along, though, I got a business ta run. Ok?" and he leaves to return to the front of his shoppe.

As they get themselves together and start to move away from the baker's wall, Charlie and Evie are really anxious to feed again after getting each other worked up. They quickly head over to The Flying Horse, hand in hand and move around to the back door, open it and go through.

"Good afternoon, Jenna," Charlie calls to the cook, who is plucking chickens at the sink. "Do ya have anything for us?"

"Just got it in a little while ago," she says, "three pots in the root cellar. Help yerself."

They rush to the root cellar and each take up a pot, draining the contents in one long gulp. At once, they feel much more "human", their eyesight clears and their teeth return to their regular length. They also notice five wrapped bundles along side the last full blood-pot.

"Pardon, Jenna," Evie enquires, poking her head from still inside the root cellar, "wot's in them packages, then, love?"

"Yes, yes, it's new gizzards from Mr. Boyle." She explains, "you can have two of tha five, but I need tha rest for me pies."

"Many thanks, Jenna," Charlie tells her. "As always, we're very appreciative."

"No worries, Charlie," Jenna replies, "you, too Evie. Now that yer more respectful."

"We've gotta get going, Jenna," Charlie explains, "we've gotta help Brien and the professor from London because Susie from The White Star got killed last night as well, and there's some new information that we've been asked to suss out."

"Well, good luck with that," she says, plucking another chicken, "let us know how ya get on, 'en, love."

Charlie picks up the full blood-pot and Evie collects the two packages and they say their good-byes to Jenna as they leave through the pub's back door. They walk down High Pavement past Stoney Street, which would take them to Charlie's house. They carry on High Pavement, which turns into Low Pavement, where the buildings become less and less frequent. Soon they were walking, hand in hand, of course, on a dirt road with hedgerows on each side.

"Now, where were we, 'fore we were so rudely interrupted?" Evie asks. She yanks Charlie's arm and pulls him through the hedgerows, which nearly causes him to spill the contents of his pot.

"Careful, love," he admonishes her. "We haven't got any more till tomorrow, you know." And he puts down the pot next to the gizzard packages that Evie has put in the grass nearby. He then tugs her hair behind her neck and pulls down her puffy top, exposing her breast's erect nipples. Evie snarls in delight as she unties Charlie's trousers.

He bites her left nipple hard and she cries out as she squeezes his erect organ. He is the one crying out now and snarling, teeth bared, head back. He tugs at Evie's skirt, discovering it's still tied at the waist. Undaunted, Charlie lifts her skirt and smells her fanny, oosing her liquid of pleasure. It is fortunate that the rain and rural location of their sexing have kept any "nosy neighbours" from finding them in their passionate and animalistic state. The vampyric couple roll over and over, first Charlie in control, as he tugs and scratches are Evie's body until she is on all fours with him kneeling behind her, keeping her fanny exposed by placing his knees between her bent legs as he enters her, pulling her hair again. Then Evie moves so that Charlie's organ becomes dislodged and she is able to shift positions so that *she* is now on top, thrusting her dripping sex organ onto his. She pinches her own nipples with one hand and plays with her clit with the other, reaching at least three orgasms before he explodes inside her, they both scream at the top of their lungs, fangs exposed, as she collapses on top of him, kissing him deeply. In short order, they each take a package and consume the contents inside, whereby their faces return to what the rest of Nottingham would consider as normal.

After they tie their clothing back in place and adjust what needs adjusting, Charlie carries the blood-pot whilst still holding Evie's hand and they carry on along their path. The no sooner hit the dirt road again, when Evie stops dead in her tracks.

"Did ya see that, love?" Evie says, looking at the ground.

"I do now, love." He agrees. And he puts down the pot, leans over and picks up what to an average human looks like a useless chunk of metal. However, to an Observant, this piece's one shiny surface beside the dingey other ones is clear to see, even amid the other pieces of metal, glass and manure on the road. It also has a unique "L-shape", with the shiny side on one face of the "L", that looks oddly familiar.

"I wonder..." Charlie says to her. "put it into your purse, sweetheart. We'll take it to Brien and the professor and see what they have to say. There can't be much more left to the print we found at the scene, but maybe this will help somehow."

"That's a good idea, love," Evie agrees, putting the metal shard into her purse.

Charlie picks up the pot again and hand-in-hand, the couple turn around and head back to where they left the constable and the professor. But, when they arrive, neither of them are to be seen.

"Maybe they went back to the professor's room?" Charlie surmises, and the pair head off to the White Star Inn, Charlie still clutching the blood pot under his arm.

Once they arrive, they are greeted by both Davy and Janie, who come rushing up to the pair.

"Oi, you two," Davy says, very excited, "Wait'll ya hear, that perfesser made a print of tha horseshoe. Said he took tha papier mache, poured it into tha hoofprint and let it set, and when he took it out, there was a perfect mould of tha horseshoe, missin' bit and all!"

"Well, Davy, love," Evie says, reaching into her purse. "I'm only guessin' that *this* is tha missin' piece o' tha' horseshoe."

"You jammy git," says a wide-eyed Janie. "Where on earth did ya find it?" She had been standing behind Davy letting him carry on with most of the conversation.

Charlie and Evie give each other a sly smile, wondering how to explain that after their intense and, border-line dangerous, love-making, they just happened upon a key piece of evidence that just might break this mystery!

"Kinda just come up on it, ya might say," Evie relates, never taking her eyes off of Charlie, returning the piece of horseshoe to her purse.

"Good job yer an Observant, then ain't it, Evie?" Janie chimes in. "Otherwise, ya probably had missed it."

"You're right, there, love," adds Charlie. "Our Evie is quite a catch, all right." And he gives her a squeeze around her bare waist. They never cease looking longingly at each other.

"Well, you'd best 'ead on upstairs, then," says Davy. "Tha perfesser and constable will be waitin' on ya. I'll watch this for ya, and I've got another one in spare for ya, as now I know that ya need 'em." And he takes the blood pot off of Charlie and heads to the back room of the bar as Charlie and Evie turn and head up the stairs to the professor's room. They arrive on the landing to the second floor and knock at the door. Hearing voices, they can tell the investigators are indeed inside.

"Entré," calls the professor's voice. And Charlie follows Evie into the room, where they find the professor discussing their findings over the papier mache casting of the hoofprint he created at the crime scene.

"And see here, the missing piece is smooth on one end, which means that it had to be sheared off by something sharp and penetrating. The poor horse must have been in extreme discomfort as he or she ran off." The Professor tells the constable.

"Yes, indeed, my good sir" the constable concurs. "Now, what we have ta do is find out who as a horse in need of shoeing. And we got our man."

"Not only that, but see what we have," Charlie says and Evie takes the horseshoe piece out of her purse again.

"I'm so excited ta see if it'll fit," she says, and places the metal into the space left in the impression. With a little adjustment in the impression and turning the piece this way and that, the smooth end fits exactly into the space left by the impression. "Ooooh, I knew it were tha right one!" she squeals.

"Yes, yes, it's quite thrilling, my dear." says the professor, placidly. "Have you a blacksmith in town, then, my good man?" he asks of the constable. "Maybe there's an opportunity of finding out who has asked to have some shoeing done."

"Certainly," Charlie chimes in. "And ironically, his name is Mr. Steele."

"Yes, that certainly is a good joke," remarks the professor.

"He used ta see both Nancy an' Susie; when they was still with us." Evie adds. "They both said 'e was *very* vigorous!" And with that, she cuddles on Charlie's shoulder as he replaces his arm around her bare waist. "'Course, he is amazingly strong, workin' metal an' all, so I wouldn't wind 'im up. Good job he don't get eggy."

"No worries, Evie," says the constable, "we'll handle him carefully. But we do have to find out if there's anyone who's gettin' their bobbo re-shod."

"Well, constable," asks the professor, "shall we go and see him now?"

"No time like tha present," Constable Waterstone answers. "Care to come along?" he asks Charlie and Evie. "Who knows wot ya might find."

"We'd love to come along," Charlie answers, and looks down at Evie at his shoulder, "unless *you've* got something else planned, love."

"Not that I can think of just now," she answers, and gives him a wry smile. "'Course I can always think of something." And the professor and the constable each look at each other, and give a knowing, slightly embarrassed smile.

"I think we can handle that in a bit, love," Charlie whispers in her ear, "after all, we just had a session a short while ago."

"I know, love," she whispers back, "but I can always use another." And raises and lowers her eyebrows lustfully.

"Later, love, later," he tells her. "Gentlemen, shall we go?"

The professor gethers up some of his belongings off of the bed, places them in his carry-bag, then follows the constable out the door, with the two vampyres following the pair as they descend the stairs and start to head out of the pub. However, as the constable opens the door, the afternoon sun gleams in. It's a good job that Charlie and Evie are following because, seeing the sunshine, they stop dead in their tracks, before the inevitable consequence occurs.

"Hold on there, you two," calls Davy from behind the bar, as the group of four stop dead in their tracks. "I got something for ya," and quickly, Davy dashes behind the bar area, through the leather curtain. He returns with two long hooded cloaks: one royal blue, the other a deep crimson. "I thought you could use something like this. So I arsed Janie ta make two o' these cloaks. She also made tha hoods extra long so you could go out in tha daylight without it causin' ya harm."

"May I have tha red one, love?" Evie asks, taking that one out of Davy's arms, pulling it over her head and pulling down the hood, "'course, it ain' quite form-fittin' is it?" and she twirls so that the edges of the cloak swirl up. "On tha other hand, nothin' says I gotta wear anything under-neath..." and looks wickedly at Charlie.

"You are incorrigible!" he tells her, laughingly, and pulls his blue cloak on. Indeed the hood is extremely long, so that his face is completely obscured.

"Davy, Janie, we can't thank you enough. These are spectacular." He says to the pair. "We'll be back for our other presents later, Davy, yeah?" then to the professor and constable. "Well, I guess that sorts it, let's off, then."

With their coverings now in place, he and Evie follow Constable Waterstone and Professor McWilliams out the door. They notice that the sleeves of their robes are also long enough to cover their hands. The only negative is that the temperature outside has also risen with the increase in sunshine, so that now it's reached the high 20 degrees and under the heavy cloaks, its even warmer, but, surprisingly to Charlie, his skin temperature is still cold and clammy.

They walk two-by-two down High Pavement and carry on along to Low Pavement, the same way that Charlie and Evie had just come. They pass the hedgerows where they had just relieved their passion, and give each other a quick giggle.

"You two, all right?" asks the constable, still walking.

"Oh, yeah," Evie says, still smiling, "just a little joke between us."

They carry on until they see the smoke coming from the blacksmith's shop. Despite the weather, there's always work for the hardest worker in town. As they approach, they hear the clang-clang of the hammer on anvil and see the large man underneath the wide overhang in front of his home, with the coal fire going, and the cask of water just next to it. He's working on some metal tool they can't see until they're within two metres of the shop itself.

"Mr. Steele," calls the constable, startling the blacksmith. He's so intent on his work that he doesn't even notice the party approaching. If Constable Waterstone is large, Mr. Iain Steele is enormous, with jet black hair and beard. He is dressed in a cotton vest and short trousers. He has enormous hands and arms the size of a lamb leg, extremely broad shoulders and a waist as small as Charlie's. His physical form looks like it's been chiselled from granite by a sculptor's impression of an inverted pyramid, and he has thighs and calves that any ox would be proud of.

"Oh, hiya constable, you ok?" asks the blacksmith, putting down his hammer and holding his hand out to shake. The constable's hand almost disappears with Mr. Steele's mammoth one as they shake their greeting. "Who's this, then?" he asks nodding toward the professor.

"This is Professor McWilliams," explains the constable, "he's visiting from London, and 'he's helping all of us look into tha murders that you no doubt heard about."

"I did indeed, Brien. Perfessa, eh?" says Mr. Steele, looking surprised. "Well, mate, you ok?" and holds out his hand to the visitor.

"I'm fine, my good man and you?" the professor's hand gets swallowed up all the way up the wrist by the huge man.

"Jus' fine, mate. Hiya, Charlie, Evie, is that you? You ok?" he acknowledges their presence. Charlie moves underneath the overhang and takes down his hood, Evie moves next to him and does the same. He also shakes the large blacksmith's hand, but with Evie, he picks her up with one arm and sits her on his right shoulder. Her long dark red hair scraping the top of the overhang.

"Oop, sorry, love," Mr. Steele says, letting her down gently. "Say Charlie, you ok? Yer hand's are ice cold on this hot day."

"Oh, no, Mr. Steele," Charlie replies, "I'm fine."

"So, gents... an' lady," he says smiling at Evie. "How c'n I help?"

The professor explains about the hoofprint, the imprint and the missing piece that Charlie and Evie found.

"Well, that's some good news, lads," says the smithee. "I would love ta know who done in our Nancy and poor Susie. I hopes you find 'em before I do," he says with fire in his eyes. As he picks up the hammer and strikes it on the anvil with such force that a shower of sparks emits from the contact. They suddenly remember what Evie had told them about getting on Mr. Steele's wrong side.

"I'm sorry," Mr. Steele says, sadly, "but, I misses them two, I do. They was nice ladies ta me."

"O' course they were," Evie says, calming him. "An' you were always nice ta them, as well, love"

"Whatever ya needs, just call on me," says the blacksmith.

"As a matter of fact," says the constable, "is there anyone who's asked ya ta make new horseshoes for 'em?"

"Yeaaaah," says Mr. Steele, scratching his beard, "I wrote it down so I wouln't forget. Have a sit." And he leaves to get his appointment list.

He returns in short order with the list in hand. "Got it!" He says. "Now, let's see, there's Watchman Masterson, Mrs. *Powers*" and the big man rolls his eyes, "oh, yeah Mikey an' Jenna come in, an' Tha Summers, Tha Logans, an' Tha Bowies. Ass ih."

"Well, that brings the list of almost a thousand townspeople down to six," says Charlie.

"An' it cuts down on who we gotta talks to", says Evie, cheerily. "makes things all right."

"Many thanks to you, Mr. Steele," says Constable Waterstone, shaking the big man's hand as they depart. "We've gotta be on our work, now, an' we know you gotta do as well."

"You're right, Brien," says the blacksmith. "I gotta get this plow back ta Tha Logans as well... eh, maybe I c'n be a constable taday as well, yeah?" he says excitedly.

"That would be wonderful, Mr. Steele," says the professor, "I'm staying at The White Star Inn, please find us there when you have enquired on the Logan family."

"'Course, I'll find you lot, no worries," he says, "but I bess finish this bafore I cleans up and goes over."

"Good luck, my good man," the professor tells him, and his hand is enveloped again.

"Tarrah, Iain," says Evie to the blacksmith and kisses his cheek, then pulls the hood over her head.

"Cheers, mate," says Charlie and pulls his hood aloft.

"Goo' luck ta you lot, as well," Mr. Steele calls in return and goes back to his tool-making with renewed vigor.

"Well, that was a well-done," says Constable Waterstone, and the quartet start off on their continuing investigation.

Chapter 22

THE SIX SUSPECTS

"Who should we see first," asks Evie.

"I'm thinking of Bill," says the constable, "I can't believe he had anything ta do wiff it, but he was tha first on tha scene for each one."

It's a short walk to Bill Masterson's house, a small thatch-covered brick home, with an overgrown walkway, and garden that is aslo in need of attention. Constable Waterstone knocks at the door and hears, "Just a mo'," from inside. The door opens and the watchman is stood there in just a dressing gown.

"Wow, constable, perfessa, Charlie, Evie, how ya goin on then?" the watchman asks.

"May we come inside?" asks the constable, sternly.

"'Course you c'n all come in. Am I in trouble, constable?" Masterson asks. "I din't do nuffin." And he looks on the verge of tears as he shows his guests into his home. "Please have a sit." And points to the four chairs surrounding the kitchen table in the front room.

Each of them take up a chair, Evie and Charlie taking off their cloaks and sit next to each other, holding hands and the constable and professor across from them.

"Now *you* behave," Charlie whispers to Evie, who looks disappointed with a pouty bottom lip.

"So, constable," says the watchman, visibly upset, "what'd I do? How c'n I fix it?"

"You're not in trouble," says Constable Waterstone, "not yet, at least. Buh you've gotta answer my questions honestly, Bill."

"'Course, 'course," the watchman says quickly, almost blubbering.

"Now, Bill, you were the first one at each of the murda scenes, yeah?" asks the constable.

"That's right," says the watchman, looking from one face to the next. "I 'eard a scream an' I went runnin'. I *am* a watchman after all."

"That's why it's so hard ta ask ya these questions," the constable relates, "we also understand that you've gotta horse what needs new shoes."

"That's right, but what's that gotta do with anything?" the watchman asks tearily, "My horse ain't done nuffin' either."

"No, but there was a hoofprint left at the scene," explains the professor, "and it was missing a horseshoe. We checked with Mr. Steele, and you asked to have him make a horseshoe for you. You can see why we are asking."

"Yeah, I asked him ta make me two new ones 'cause my horse wore out his back two as we was all over town bein' tha watchmnan," Masterson explains, "an' I ain't as small as I use ta be." And pats his rather large middle. "But, I swears, constable, it's not my horse yer lookin' for."

"Then, Bill, you won't mind if we have us a look-see in yer stable, yeah?"

"No, *sir*," he agrees, "I'll take ya ta see Scratcher. You'll see for yerself." And he puts on his floppy Watchman's hat and leads the team out of his house.

They walk around the house to the barn that the houses in the community all belong to. The front of the stalls are marked with the names of the horses and their owners. The walk along behind Watchman Masterson past the first three stalls ont he left and right before stopping at the fourth stall on the left. The signs say "Scratcher" and "William Masterson". The watchman opens the stall and pets the horse on the nose, who whinnies in response. He unties the horse and moves him out of the stall, moving him past the four guests. He re-ties the horse to the next stall so that the rear is adjacent to the other four, as Scratcher swishes his tail. The watchman moves to the rear of the horse and lifts his left rear hoof. The horseshoe is worn down almost to the hoof, but there is no piece missing from it.

"See, constable, I told ya it weren't me," the watchman says almost crying his innoscence."

"That's fine, Bill," the constable replies. "Now about the other hoof, please. An' please stop scratin'. Ya ain't in no trouble, like I said."

Watchman Masterson lifts the right rear hoof only to find it completely as worn down as the left one. There is no piece missing from this one either. He then lifts up the right fore-hoof and the left fore-hoof in turn and though they have also shown wear and tear, there is much more life in them than the rear ones.

"See, constable," sniffles the watchman, "I told ya, I told ya. But, I knew ya had ta look inta it... an' me, 'course now that I know what ya found."

"It's all right, now Billy," Evie tells him. "We just had ta check everyone what had a horse in needa shoein'."

Watchman Masterson composes himself as best he can, wiping his tears and his runny nose on the right sleeve of his dressing gown, sniffling and easing his crying, but calming down slowly.

"So, where ya off to next, then?" asks the watchman, "An' can I help at all?"

"Actually, yeah," says the constable, "you can go to The Bowie's family, they also got a horse in needa shoein'."

"Just make sure ya treat 'em as nice as we did you, Bill," Charlie reminds him. "Gee, I guess I'm more famished than I thought. C'mon, Evie, maybe we'd bess get back to Tha White Star. Davy got that present fer us."

"That's a good idea, you two," the constable agrees. "You go on, now an' get yer gift."

"Wha you going on abou'?" asks sthe watchman. "What's wiff you two? An' I ain't deard nuffin about no gifts. Is it yer birthday, Evie? Charlie? I din't getcha nuffin!"

The four look at each other and give a slight smile as Charlie and Evie replace their hoods and turn and leave the barn.

"We'll meet you at the Summers' farm when you're done," Constable Waterstone calls to them.

"No one *told* me," is the last thing the vampyric pair hear as they turn their attention to the roads back to the pub and their nourishment. They move quickly and silently to the White Star Inn, seeing redder and redder and their teeth getting longer and longer each second. By the time they arrive, their truly are famished for blood. As soon as they enter the pub, Davy leads them back behind the curtain, where the pot from The Flying Horseman sits on a shelf next to the one Davy saved for them. They leave their hoods up over their faces so as not to alarm the guests. Charlie and Evie each greedily grab a pot off the shelf and eagerly finish off the contents; which immediately returns their facial dimensions back to their normal constitution.

"Well, we'd better get back and meet Brien and the professor at the Summers'," Charlie tells Evie. We might also see how Mr. Steele and Bill have got on with their enquiries."

"All right, love," Evie replies, and the two say their thanks to Davy and Janie, who's waiting on a table containing one of the girls and a very amorous customer sat next to her, then pull up their hoods and head off just a quickly and silently as they arrived.

They stop back at Charlie's, hook up Chauncy to the carriage and head off to the west side of town to get to the Summers' farmhouse. They arrive just as Professor McWilliams and Constable Waterstone dismount from their own carriage.

"It took a while to get Bill back to himself, dressed and ready to go to the Bowies'," the constable relates. "I only hope he can get some descent questions answered. We had ta give 'im tha questions ta ask." And the four of them laugh together as they walk up the path to the house.

"Constable," asks the professor, "are you sure *you* know what questions to ask *this* family?"

"Why perfessa," retorts the constable, "if I didn't know better, I would have thought you were gettin' a sence of humour." And he knocks at the door.

"Who tha fuck..." they hear a voice bellow from behind the door.

"Looks like Ol' Man Summers is at it again," says Evie. "when he were single, he useta beat up tha girls as he were doin' 'em. That's why none a 'em would go with 'im anymore. Then he got married, an' from what I hears, he now takes it out on 'er. She were brought up in it, so didn't know nuffin' different."

The door lurches open and a wiry man of average height glares at them from inside the house. He has a thin beard and shaved head and his knuckles show the scars of an abuser.

"What you want then, constable," says the man with a defiant sneer at the title. "there ain' nuffin' goin' on here."

"Who is it, love?" asks a squeaky voice from somewhere inside.

"Shut yer gob," Mr. Summers shouts at his wife. "it's got nuffin' ta do with you... or it betta not." Then back to the visitors at his door, "get on with it, then, I got business ta take care of with me missus."

"We were told that you have a horse in need of shoeing." Says the constable.

So what if I have?" Mr. Summers asks. "What is that ta you lot? Oh, an' I see ya got one o' them tarts with ya. What you want with this, then, ya slag!"

"You can take it back, or we can settle this here and now," Charlie tells him. "And I am not your wife or another girl, I can tell *you*." And his eyes are burning red despite his just feeding. But Mr. Summers just got to him with his one rude comment toward his lover as well as his reputation.

"Oh, we might just, mate," says Mr. Summers, shrugging his shoulders. "But not just yet. So, get on with it, what about my horse?"

"We found a clue as to who is killin' tha girls in town, an' it has ta do with a horse with one bad shoe." The constable explains.

"Well, ain't that too bad," says the man, unsympathetically. "Slags gettin' killt. Tsk-tsk-tsk."

"We'd really appreciate it, my good man, if you could let us look at your horses to... eliminate you as a suspect," the professor chimes in.

"An' who might you be, sweetheart," Mr. Summers sneers at the professor. "another o' them clients o' *that* tart?" Charlie takes another step in Summer's direction.

"Charlie, calm down," Constable Waterstone tells him, as if he could actually hold him back.

"I swear, matey," says Charlie to the man, "you say one more word about our Evie an' I'll rip your head off."

"Don't wind 'im up, darlin'," says the squeaky voice once more.

"I told you ta shut yer pie-hole," Mr. Summers shouts at his wife again. Then, he walks quickly back into the house. Suddenly the four at the door hear two loud slaps followed by a thud as Mrs. Summers apparently has hit the floor and Mr. Summers yelling "when I say somethin, ya better lissen, or I'll beat ya till you can't stand up. An' then where'll you be, eh? Right back where I found ya. With yer piss-head of an ol' man what beat ya every night! An' keep them kids under control bafore I beat them as well!"

"Mr. Summers, would you come here, sir," asks the constable.

The man returns to the doorway, where the constable is standing arms folded across his chest. "Firstly, sir, if I see you hit your wife again, I will most definitely arrest you and throw ya in jail until I can get a judge here, which *may* be next month or so. And secondly, can we see yer horses or not?"

"*No*! You cannot." He says, "an' how I treats me property is my own affairs, now get off my property an' stay off." And with that, Mr. Summers slams the door in their faces.

"Well, I guess that's it for now," says the professor. Charlie is still worked up and Evie is irate.

Constable Waterstone is frustrated and angry, "He does my 'head in, he does. But that doesn't mean we gotta do whatever *he* says. *We* ain't married ta 'im!"

With that, the constable turns on his heels and heads to the Summers' hay barn where he figures the horses are kept. Fortunately, there are only two to inspect. There's the family horse that they take to town pulling the carriage, and the plowhorse that works the field.

"Well, let's get to it, then," says the professor, "before he decides to check on us, after all, our carriages are still out front."

Quickly, the professor and constable inspect the plow horse and after examining each hoof, conclude that it's not this horse that is in need of a new horseshoe. Simultantously, Charlie and Evie take the family horse and there's the left rear hoof that is also missing a piece of the horseshoe, however, the missing piece is in the middle of the shoe, rather than at the end where their piece fits. So, as much as they would like it to be, Mr. Summers is ruled out, at least of this crime. They rush their way back up the pathway away from the house to their carriages and climb aboard.

"Let's go to Tha Flying Horse an' have a chin-wag with Mikey an' Jenna." Constable Waterstone tells them as they gallop their horses and carriages away from the Summers farm.

The quartet travel back into town and stop at The Flying Horse. They see both Mikey and Jenna in the front of the bar. Mikey is pulling pints and Jenna is running to and from the back of the bar, giving drinks and food to the patrons of the busy pub.

"Can we talk ta ya both?" asks the constable. "There's a mtter we need ta talk about."

"'Course," says Mikey, "Jenna?" he calls and she comes out from the back of the bar where the kitchen is. "They wanna have a chat with both of us."

"What's this about, Brien?" asks Jenna.

"Well, Jenna," the constable begins, "it's no secret that you don't think too much o' tha girls round here."

"'At's right, an' I'm not tha only one," she comes back with, "there's lots o' folks that don't like them tarts. Mostly wives what got husbands who are bein' asked all tha time ta have a go with 'em. Spendin' money, time, an' lovin' on 'em, instead o' their woman at 'ome."

"Well, my dear," says the professor, "I can certainly understand your and others concern. However, when some of these, tarts, as you put it, get murdered, well, then a certain amount of suspicion will fall on you."

"Now Jenna," says Charlie, "we're not saying that you had anything to do with these nasty things, but you can see how it looks, don't ya?"

"Yeah, Charlie, I can see all righ'," Jenna agerees, "but I been here every time one o' them tarts got 'erself killt. You was here when Nancy got done in, Evie. An' my Mikey here were here fer all tha other ones."

"'At's righ', Brien," Mikey confirms, "an' you know how honest I am, mate."

"'Course, I know Mikey," the constable says, "but yer man ain't exackly tha most impartial witness, Jenna, love, plus, Mikey, you coulda done 'em for yer bird. An' then there's tha matter of that horse."

"Oi, what about tha 'orse?" Mikey asks.

"Tha perfessa, here, found a hoofprint and I found tha missin' piece, which we're tryin' ta find tha owner," Evie explains, "so if we can just look at yer horse's hoofs so we can take ya off our list, please."

"Well, since ya put it *that* way," Jenna says. "Mikey, can you bring 'em round ta tha stables, love? I've gotta finish makin' them pies, an' cuttin' tha bread, an' makin' tea, I just can't, sweetheart."

"'Course, Jenna," Mikey replies, "c'mon you lot, let's take us off that list, then." And he leads them out the front door of the pub, take a left around the building and to the small rear stables, where there's a black carriage parked in front. They walk through the open barn door and pass two empty stalls, one on each side. In the next set of stalls, however, there's a horse on each side, a grey, large one on the right, who comes to the front of the stall as the five visitors approach.

"'At's Raindrop, he's very friendly," Mikey tells the other four, "He'll let ya pet 'im an' everything."

Evie is the first one to step up and pet Raindrop on the nose, he whinnies in gleeful response. The horse then looks at the others, who each step up in turn to pet him.

All right, then, how this is not Raindrop, what needs a new shoe, but if ya wanna see his `oofs, ya certainly can." Mikey tells them. With that, he leads the horse out of the stall and surely, his horseshoes are slightly worn, but not enough to need new ones. Mikey replaces Raindrop back in his stall, and they move to the stall across the way.

"This is tha one what needs a new shoe," Mikey informs them, "This is Biscuit." This horse is a tall, thinner, deep brown male with a white stripe down the length of his nose. "He's not as friendly as Raindrop, but he's not mean at all." He goes into the stall and brings the horse out for his inspection. The horse shakes his head, but is not bothered, just as Mikey had told them. Mikey then lifts each hoof in turn, and the right fore-hoof is the one that needs re-shoeing. There's a piece missing form it, on one edge, but as was the case with Mr. Summers' horse, the piece in Evie's purse is no match for the shoe that needs replacing.

"Thank you Mikey," the constable tells him, "now we can eliminate you, and Jenna, as suspects in the murders. And for me, I'm really grateful. It would have been horrible ta have ta put eitha o' you in the Nick."

"Glad 'bout that as well," Jenna says. "Well, carry on, then, you lot. I 'ope ya can catch who done it. Tarrah, all."

"Tarrah, then Jenna," says Charlie. And the four of them turn and go as Jenna heads out of the barn with them and turns to go back to the pub.

"So, I guess we need to go back to The White Star and see how the others have got on." The professor says.

"We just 'ave one more stop ta make b'fore that," Constable Waterstone tells them, "we're in tha neighbourhood, so might as well. It's Mrs. Powers, an' she can be right munky. Maybe even worser than Mr. Summers back there."

"You're right on that score, constable," says Charlie, "if I'm not spot-on with the rent, she runs me up one side and down the other. So, it only happened once, I can tell ya."

An' I already know what she thinks o' us girls," Evie adds. "she ain't tha only one, like Jenna said, but she don't like us by no account."

"Well," the constable replies, "'at's enough for me, let's go." And he and the professor climb aboard their carriage, whilst Charlie and Evie do the same on theirs, silently.

They ride back along High Pavement, turn on Stoney Street and ride past Charlie's house. They ease up to Mrs. Powers' path between the split-rail fence surrounding her home and tie both horses to one of the vertical rails. They four move up to the front doot and Constable Waterstone knocks.

"Who is it?" says an eggy female voice from inside. "I ain't openin' tha door for no one, less I know who ya are."

"It's Contable Waterstone, Mrs. Powers, we have some questions for ya." He says in return. "Mind, you might open tha door for us."

I ain't got nuffin' ta say, `cause I ain't done nuffin' wrong, constable." says the voice.

"Would you mine openin' tha door, please, Mrs. Powers?" the constable asks again.

"Fine, fine," she says and opens the door. She is dressed in a long-sleeved floor-length house dress with a flour-spotted apron over it. She stands there arms folded across her chest, defiantly. "Ayup, Charlie. I see yer still with that trollop. An' who might *he* be?" she asks and nods toward the professor.

"I'm Professor McWilliams, Mrs. Powers. I've come from London to help with the murders that have been happening around here." He explains.

"Look, we don't need no fancy thinkin-man from Tha Big Smoke up here muckin' things up," she sneers at the professor, "our constable can handle things just fine. Can't ya, constable."

"Another set o' eyes couldn't `urt." the constable tells her, "'specially since he has more experience with murdas than I do."

"So, what ya doin' here then, an' don't *you* say nuffin, missy," she says to Evie. "Like I said, I ain't done nuffin'."

"We understand that one o' yer horses needs new shoes," Evie tells her, "we just wanna have an eyeball."

"I told *you* ta shut yer gob, ya twat," glares Mrs. Powers at Evie. "You ain't havin' a look at nuffin'!"

"I *am* the constable for all of Nottingham, Mrs. Powers," reminded Constable Waterstone, "an' I have tha authority ta look anywhere I wanna."

Mrs. Powers moves away from the doorway, back into the house, surprisingly quickly for an older woman, she grabs a cast-iron fry pan from the rack above the hob. She turns back to the doorway and throws the pan directly at the constable's head. He ducks behind the doorframe just as the pan goes whizzing by, barely missing the professor. But Charlie, even with the hood covering his head, catches the fry pan by the handle as it comes tumbling.

"I don't care what kinda authority ya think ya have," she screamed at him, "ya can't just go botherin' an 'elpless ol' woman, like this."

"Mrs. Powers..." begins the constable.

She throws a cast iron sauce pan this time, this time caught by Evie as the professor has cowered behind the two vampyres. "Get outta here," screams Mrs. Powers, "an' don't you come back! An' don't worry, I'll be watchin'. I got nephews an' I'm tellin' 'em ta come over, as I need pertection from yer harrassin' me."

"Mrs. Powers, that won't be necessary," says the professor, peeking from behind Charlie's shoulder. "I'm sure the constable here, can see that a fragile old woman, such as you, is incapable of these vicious crimes."

"Is that so?" asks Mrs. Powers, raising another pot in hand, ready to launch it at the visitors at her door again.

"I... I suppose so, Mrs. Powers," says the constable, "I believe I can take your name off the list of those we suspect of murda."

"'At's fine, constable," she says, "now get outta here b'fore I don't miss ya with tha next' one. An' I am still goin' ta have my nephews come over fer pertection."

"You can do what you want," pipes in Evie, "but just know, my Charlie 'n' me, we ain't done with you by a long stride."

"Well *you 'n' Charlie* can just go ta hell, for all I care," quipped Mrs. Powers in return, weaving a wooden spoon in the pair's direction. "'Cause ya keep this up, an' you 'n' Charlie can fine another place ta live, if ya calls it that."

"That's all right, Mrs. Powers," says Charlie, placing the fry pan he's still holding on the ground just ouside the door to her house. Evie follows suit with the sauce pan that she's holding. The professor and constable look at each other curiously. Mrs. Powers then moves to the door.

"You four can just get off my lands, now," she scolds them, "I got a lotta pans here, you lot."

"Thank you for your 'elp, Mrs. Powers," says the constable. And as Mrs. Powers slams the door in their faces, the constable, the professor and Charlie and Evie are walking back up the path to where their carriages are located.

"All right, we can 'ead on back to Tha White Star, now," says the constable. "I know, we ain't seen tha horses, but I don't think that tha murdas were done by that ol' woman."

"That's what you think, but we need to be sure," the professor answers. "Can we come back later or tomorrow?"

"Charlie 'n' I can," replies Evie. "After all, we don't need ta sleep, ya know." And she gives a little squeeze to Charlie's arm as he looks affectionately down at her.

"Well, before you two go off 'n'do what you do," the constable replies, "let's see what tha others found out."

Chapter 23

BACK AT THE WHITE STAR

The two carriages then take off from Mrs. Powers', head up Stoney Street and turn onto High Pavement stopping in back of the White Star Inn. It's just past 17:00 when they arrive back at the pub. The constable and professor tie their horse up on one of the railings attached to the barn. Charlie and Evie do the same to another post.

"I'll tell Davy and Janie that we're back," says the constable, "he'll put the horse an' carriage away proper." And they head inside. Charlie and Evie take down the hoods on their cloaks. At the bar are both Watchman Masterson and Mr. Steele having a pint and talking enthusiastically.

"Hiya, Davy, can you see to the 'orse an' carriage, then, mate?" asks Constable Waterstone.

"No worries, constable," says the barman, "I'll see to it."

"Ayup, you two," Constable Waterstone addresses the pair, "so what have you got on about?"

"Well, we've got some news, mind," answers the watchman, "but it may not be tha kint ya want."

"Let us retire upstairs to my room and discuss this away from prying ears," says the professor. The two drinking gents finish their pints then join the quartet and head up to the professor's room.

Arriving at the landing of the second floor, Professor McWilliams lets them inside.

"So, what did you two gentlemen find out?" asks the professor.

"I went to tha Logans an' checked out their 'orses," said the blacksmith, "an' all o' 'em had shoes worn down to tha nubs. Now, mind, I ain't seen 'em in quite a while, so, it's not a surprise that they need shoes, all o' 'em. I'm just happy that they'll be comin' ta me ta have 'em done."

"Who else in town'd they come to, Mr.Steele?" asks the constable, "yer tha only smithy in this whole part o' town, mate." And he laughs heartily along with the blacksmith. "What 'bout you, Bill, what you found?"

The watchman looks down sheepishly, "Well, constable," he stammers, "ya see, there was Mrs. Bowie, an' I went ta school with 'er, she were mean then, an' she ain't got no better since. I feel sorry for our poor Mr. Bowie, 'e got ta put up with 'er every day, sir. Well, she wouldn't let me see nuffin o' them `orses. An' she had a kitchen knife big as one o' 'em soldier's swords! I weren't gonna do nuffin wiffout you, an' Charlie, and Evie along with me."

"Bill, you are twice 'er size, mate," reminded the constable, as Charlie and Evie look at each other and laugh under their breaths at the absurdity of the situation, "an' you couldn't just ask *Mr.* Bowie?"

"As I said, sir," the watchman continues, "'E's just as scared as I were. An' 'e's gotta live with 'er. I can see why they ain't got no kids. Who'd wanna have ta put up with 'er as a mum?"

"Well, it's getting late," says the professor, "and I need to have tea. Wonder what Janie has made up tonight?"

"S'all right, perfessa," the watchman says, "I think I'll join ya, if 'at's ok, mate."

"Don't know how you could be 'ungry already," Evie tells him, "after all, Mrs. Bowie nearly took yer 'ead off, love." And Watchman Masterson looked down in embarrassment, whilst the teasing Evie smiled amusedly. Then, seeing how her words affected the poor man, Evie says, "Aww, I didn't mean nuffin, love. I was just takin' tha piss. You did yer job right, Billy. Look, ta fix this, I'll speak ta tha girls an' have one of 'em have tea with you two. Then, you can see 'er after that... private like, ok?"

"Cheers, Evie, that would be really nice," sniffles the watchman, "I gets a li'l sensative 'bout my position as watchman for tha town. An', now just as tha constable gave me a real important job ta do, I didn't go an' do it right. I let Mrs. Bowie get tha best o' me, jus' like at school."

"Well, Bill," says Charlie, "truth be told, Mrs. Powers got the best of us as well. Guess they're two peas in the pod, yeah?"

"Well, Charlie, that makes me feel a li'l better," the watchman replies, "But, yer right, mate, them two are frightnin'." And the watchman, constable and Charlie and Evie all laugh.

"Well, we'll be off, then, yeah?" says Evie, "me 'n' Charlie got our jobs ta do after we have a bit o' tea ourselves."

"Tarrah, then you two," the constable tells them. "Let us know what you find back at the Bowies, ok?"

"Though' we was goin' back ta Mrs. Powers," Charlie says, the days' activity clearly affecting him.

"She's such a tough one, she is" says the constable, "thought we'd... all go an' handle that one tagether, 'specially if she brings in 'er nephews. Don't want no kinda trouble with more 'n' just 'er."

"That makes sence, Brien," says Charlie, "ok, we'll go see tha Bowies, then. Maybe Mr. Bowie can get 'is wife under control, an' we can see their 'orses. After all when she caught `im with one o' *yer* friends Evie, in their own 'ome not that long ago, 'member?"

"I do, love," Evie confirmed, "an' she weren't too pleased abou' it. Said she hated us girls an' wished us all go ta hell. Jus' like Mrs. Powers done." And she sneered at the mere mention of Charlie's landlady who treated her so rudely.

Charlie could feel his teeth start to grow slightly and could see, through his crimson view, that Evie's eyes have started to go red, meaning feeding time was fast approaching.

"We'd best be on our way, lads, tarrah, then," says Evie quickly and pulls the hood back over her head, covering her changing visage, and heads for the door. Charlie pulls his hood on, and saying his "Cheers" to his comrades and leaves rapidly, following Evie, heading downstairs to see Davy and Janie as to where *their* meal might be.

"Cheers, you lot," says Watchman Masterson. "Wonder what's up with 'em two, then, yeah, constable?"

"It's complicated, Bill" says the constable. "She and Charlie have ta go now, but they'll be back later, I'm sure after they've ate. Let's go to tea, ourselves, lads."

"That sounds like a capital idea," says the professor who was still hungry from earlier. And he leads the other two gentlemen out the door and downstairs to the kitchen.

Meanwhile, Charlie and Evie have already gone to the back to find the pots of blood that Davy had kept in the root cellar for them once they returned from their day of investigation. And as usually happened prior to eating, Evie was feeling a bit randy. So after downing her nourishment, she positions herself sat against the back wall, feet wider than shoulder width apart as she gradually lifts her skirt, exposing her naked fanny. She puts her left hand to her clitoris, rubbing the bud around with her index finger. Charlie is also feeling as interested in feeding his libido as in his hunger as he undoes his trousers and they fall down to his ankles, exposing his large erection pointing straight out pointing at Evie.

"One o' these days, I'm gonna get there first." He says jokingly.

"Not bloody likely," she says back. He approaches her and falls on his knees, erection aiming at its' dripping target. She spreads herself apart with both hands, still playing with her clit with her left index finger and snarls in anticipation of the pleasure to come. He snarls back and enters her completely in one thrust. She leaves her own body and digs her fingernails into the cheeks of his arse, pulling him even deeper into her if that's possible. He growls in pleasure himself as he thrusts and thrusts and sinks his teeth into her neck. She rips at his back now and lifts her feet allowing him even more access to her inner parts and growls loudly. Until...

"Will ya keep it down!" it's Davy quickly coming through the leather curtain separating the back section from the front of the pub. "I told 'em that it were dogs fightin' over tha rats on tha rubbish pile. But, some of 'em gonna get curious, you two keep it up. Now finish wot ya come for and be done with ya."

"Sorry, Davy," says Charlie, dislodging himself from Evie, his still enlarged organ dripping with Evie's juices, and standing up to pull his trousers up once more. "Come on, love, let's feed 'n' then join with tha others."

"Ugh, I can't watch 'at," Davy says and disappears throught the leather curtain again.

"But I ain't finished yet, love," she says putting her hands to her vagina again.

"Me either, my love, but we gotta wait till we get 'ome," he tells her, "we need Davy an' Janie ta help us." And he takes up the blood-pots and hands one to Evie who is just now getting to her feet, dusting off her skirt. She takes the pot from Charlie and they both drain their pots dry. They emerge from the root cellar to find Janie coming through the curtain, carrying dirty plates piled high. She moves to the sink and places the dishes in the soapy water.

"There ya are, you two," she greets them cheerily, "don't you pay no mind ta our Davy, 'e just guess a li'l eggy when there's a commotion."

"It's all right, Janie," Charlie tells her, "we just needed some nourishment before our nightly visit and the constable has given us some work to do for him."

"So, ya feelin' better, now?" she asks.

"Yeah, Janie," Evie replies, "*almost* back ta normal," and she looks Charlie with a 'still not done yet look in her eye.

"Yeah, we 'eard you two all right," Janie says, "an ya ain't done yet? Crikies! Me 'n' Davy would o' knocked it out by this time. Hahahaha."

"So, are the others still eating?" Charlie asks her, changing the subject.

"Yeah, an' then they're goin' ta see that toss-pot Mrs. Powers again," she explains, "An' they're takin' Billy Boy with 'em. Not that tha constable can't handle things, but, just ta have one in spare."

"Well, we'd better be off ourselves, then," Charlie tells her, "we've got a job of our own to sort out. But maybe if we can take care of the Bowies, we'll pop over to Mrs. Powers and help the others."

"C'mon, love, let's off. Cheers, Janie, tell thanks ta Davy as well, me ducks," says Evie cheerily as they head through the curtain to where Chauncy is tied up with the carriage. It's still light out as they pull their hoods on again and climb into the carriage, they give Chauncy a gently snap of the reigns and head off up High Pavement, away from Stoney Street and turn onto Low Pavement and onto Centre Gate Street. There, at Number 13 is the house is the Bowie's home. A single floor building amongst the taller shops that have obviously sprung up since the house was built. There's a thatch roof and a cooking fire, probably, emitting smoke from the chimney.

Charlie decides, with the mardy mood that Mrs. Bowie was in when Watchman Masterson visited them before, to keep going until they're in front of Number 23, five houses further down Centre Gate, where there's a general post to tie Chauncy up to.

"At's smart, love," Evie tells him, reading his mind.

They tie Chauncy up to the railing on the side of the road, ans walk silently back to the path infront of Number 13. As they walk up the path, they each notice hoof prints from the house to the barn behind and again from the barn to the fields beyond that. The rainy day has provided the pair with soft wet ground that even a non-Observant would notice... maybe. But for them, it was no problem seeing that there were three different sets of tracks. The first was a large set, deeply made in the mud and only from the barn to the fields. This obviously belonged to the work-horse and the prints it made were complete, and there were even small, circular impressions made by the nails in the horseshoes. The next two sets were identical in size and travelled in front of the house as well as from the house to the barn. One set was complete, but slighty warn, as evidenced by the deeper nail holes clearly visible. The other did have a chunk missing from the print and it was on the correct side of the horseshoe. As a result, the pair make their way to the barn and with no effort at all, slide open the door and shut it behind them. In their stalls are all three horses, who whinney at the approaching vampyres. Charlie holds his hand up and immediately the horses go quiet. They hear Mrs. Bowie inside the house, "Would *you* go see what them fool 'orses are on about! Who knows, might be that someone's stealin' 'em, not that *you'd* do anything about it ya tosser."

Charlie and Evie move from the first stall on the right where the work-horse is located and they move on.

"All right, love," says the man's voice, calmly, in reply. "Let me just finish my tea, dear."

"Finish yer life, more like," yells the woman, "*Would* you go out there 'n' sort it out!"

The first stall on the left is where one of the two "town-horses" are kept. The name on the stall says, Alice. They quickly move inside the stall and inspect all four hooves, these are the worn-down ones with nails protruding from the shoes. So they close the stall door and move on.

"Just a mo', love," the husband says, trying to remain calm with a mouth full of food, which causes him to mumble his words.

"*No*, not `just a mo, love'," she screams, "you'll do it *now*." And there's a great crash as what must have been a plate gets thrown against the wall, as there's no yell of pain, it has clearly missed Mr. Bowie's head.

"All right, all right, I'll go have a look-see," says Mr. Bowie, "will 'at make you happy, love?" and the sound of a chair scraping the floor is clearly heard by the two creatures of the night as they make their way to the stall next to Alice. They open the stall door and are just about to check the first hoof when the barn door slides open and Mr. Bowie appears in the doorway. It is complete and still in good order.

"Charlie? Evie? Is `at you?" he whispers, and looks behind him in the direction of the house "what you lot doin' 'ere?"

"As you know, the constable is looking into the murders, I'm sure the watchman told you earlier," Charlie says quietly.

"Listen you better make it quick," Mr. Bowie says cautiously peering back at the house, "tha missus ain't keen on havin' no one here, an' she hates you lot." He nods to Evie. "Yeah, she told ol Billy-boy ta leave us alone in no small terms!"

"'At don't change tha fact that we need ta check yer 'orses, here," Evie tells him. "Now we seen tha other two an' they're fine, but this other one, we still need ta sort this one out. You know that 'e's missin' part o' one shoe. Now I got a missin' piece, see, an' I gotta check ta see if it fits. An' I wouldn't do nuffin ta try an' stop me. Nor tha missus either."

"You'd better get on with it then, Evie," Mr. Bowie tells her, "if she finds you 'ere, she'll be kittled... an' I'll be dead!"

Quickly and quietly, Charlie and Evie re-enter the third horses' stall and sure enough, on the left rear hoof, is a chunk missing from the shoe. Evie takes her piece out of her purse and places it into the missing part of the shoe. It's close, but the shiny side is angled in the opposite direction.

"What is up with 'em 'orses?" screaches woman's voice from the house, "Ya want me ta come and sort it out? I know how useless *you* are."

"No, 'at's all right, love," Mr. Bowie calls back, "I got 'em sorted out, just givin' 'em some oats ta ease 'em back quiet."

"Not oats, ya pratt," screams the woman, "chicory! Give 'em chickory! 'At'll quieten 'em, ya wazzuk!"

"Thank you, my love," Mr. Bowie answers. Then, whispering to the couple, "an' now that ya looked a' my 'orses, *you* best get on yer way as well b'fore she comes out here ta see what I were up to an' we're all in trouble."

"OK, love," Evie tells him, and she and Charlie pull the hoods over their heads again as they make their way out of the barn.

"Oi, who are you two?" screams Mrs. Bowie from just inside the doorway. She's a short stout woman dressed in an all-black dress, sleeves rolled up and a bloody apron at her waist, "an what you doin' in my barn, then? Where's that pie-can of a husband o' mine?"

"It's me, Charlie, Emma," he says hurridly, "we just had a question for him. He's still in the barn, sorting out the horses, dear. We gotta be on our way now. Tarrah, then." And he hustles Evie off before Mrs.

Bowie recognises her. They move quickly and silently up to Number 23, where they untie Chauncy, climb aboard the carriage and head back down Centre Gate Street in the direction from which they had come.

Chapter 24

MRS. POWERS' HOUSE

They quickly ride down Low Pavement, High Pavement and then turn onto Stoney Street again. They arrive at Mrs. Powers where she is still stood inside the open door, yelling at Constable Waterstone, Profewossor McWilliams and Watchman Masterson.

"I told ya b'fore," she's yelling at them holding her long cane by the curled end and waving it at the gentlemen at the door, "ya ain't gonna see nuffin in my barn an' `at's it."

"But Mrs. Powers, we just wanna make sure none o' your 'orses was there at tha murdahs," the watchman tells her, ducking the cane being waved in his direction.

"An' who cares if those twats got 'emselfs killt," Mrs. Powers shouts, still waving the cane wildly, "throats cut out so's they can't do nuffin with their filthy mouths."

"How did *you* know about their throats?" asks the professor, "you weren't even in on the discussions."

"I... I musta heard about it, from someone in town," Mrs. Powers stammers, suddenly seemingly less threatening than a few minutes ago as she lowers her cane.

"Can we see yer arms, Mrs. Powers," Evie says, "it's a stiflin' day fer you ta be wearin' long sleeves." And Mrs. Powers reactively pulls at her sleeves, letting go of the cane in the process. Charlie and Evie get a whiff of the indescribably delicious scent of blood as Mrs. Powers touches her arm, instinctively.

"There had to be quite a struggle those girls put up as they were killed," Charlie says, "whose traps did you use?"

"Traps, traps?" says Mrs. Powers, "who said anything 'bout traps?"

"Yes, Mrs. Powers," says the constable, "the perfessor here found that all the girls were killt with animal traps. Do you know anything about that?"

"Traps! Traps?" says Mrs. Powers, looking about suspiciously, defiantly in charge again, " I most certainly do, my lovelies, they was *my* traps an' they didn't put up much o' one after I ripped their throats out. I still got 'em traps, in my root cella. Wanna see 'em, dearie?" she says to Evie. "Washed 'em off good so's they wouldn't stink and there they are. All done and dusted."

"But, Mrs. Powers," the watchman begins, "why'd you do it?"

"Me 'usband ya see," she says, "'e spent ten pound a week on trallops. An' then one day, 'e tells me that 'e's goin off with one o' 'em ta tha Colonies... *tha Colonies*! Can you imagine?"

"I thought your husband was at sea," Charlie says, "that's what you kept telling everyone; that one day he'd be coming back."

"Had ta say somethin' didn't I?" she says, "Actually, 'e never left took care o' 'im an' 'is cunny from tha other side o' town back in March. Actually brought 'er here as 'e were packin' up, cheeky bastard. Get a new start, says 'e. Did 'em in with one o' me own kitchen knives, right cross tha throat. They're buried in tha back garden, next ta tha pea pods. 'E aways liked mushy peas for his tea, so now 'e can have 'em any time 'e likes." She says with an evil smile. "'At's how I got tha idea for tha traps, see. It were tricky slittin' their throats in tha bedroom, so he couldn't scream, but he made 'nuff noise so tha' twa' come runnin' in. Eard 'im moanin', ya see? Had ta lop off 'is bollocks an' shove 'em down 'er gob as I put tha knife in 'er gullet, then slit 'er manky throat."

"Buh how did ya manage them traps all by yerself?" asks the constable. "Even I have trouble openin' 'em proper without catchin' my fingers."

"Me dad showed me how ta use scissors ta keep it open long 'nuff ta load it proper," she explained. "Then all I had ta do was get them three trallops ta follow me inta tha jitty, tellin' 'em that they had ta see sumthin' that would make 'em lot's o' money. 'Course, they followed, all you twats want is money, an' ya don't care how ya makes it." She looks at Evie for this statement and leaps for her, suddenly holding a fully-loaded trap in her hand.

Evie, however, is quicker and in one deft move, grabs the older woman's arm and throws her over her shoulder to the ground. Mrs. Powers screams in pain as she releases her weapon with Evie still holding onto her arm, she moves swiftly on top of the older woman, knees on her upper arms now, teeth bared and eyes glowing red. Her hands go immediately to Mrs. Powers face, turning it so her neck is completely exposed. Mrs. Powers, eyes wide in frightening alarm releases a horrid scream as she realises that she is now the prey for the vampire's predatory position. There's nothing she can do but scream.

"Evie! No!" shouts Charlie, and Evie shoots him an angry look, "I know they were your friends, but let Brien and Bill take her and put her in the Nick until her trial. We've got enough to have her hang." He tells her, but she is still sat astride poor, alarmed, Mrs. Powers. "C'mon, Evie, let's go home now, you can take all this out on me."

"Don't get up yet, Evie," Constable Waterstone tells her, "let me get tha irons from my carriage first. I brought 'em just in case we fount tha killa."

Evie gradually eases up mentally, her eyes become less red and her teeth begin receding slowly. But not physically, she does not move from her positon whilst the constable runs to the carriage, removes the irons from the carriage and returns to the scene in front of Mrs. Powers' house. He clasps the iron hand clamps around her right wrist, "c'mon, Evie, I've got 'er now. Thank you, love." And Evie slowly rises from off of Mrs. Powers, who is still in a state of shock as Contable Waterstone turns her over and locks the other hand-clamp on her left wrist. He then fastens the leg-irons around each ankle. The now-shackled Mrs. Powers is lifted from the ground by both the constable and the watchman. Her expression has not changed since discovering Evie's new condition. Finally, coming to herself, she addresses the group.

"So, not only are you a walking cunny, but yer a vamp as well, eh," she says in Evie's direction, "did you know 'bout this, Charlie? 'Course ya did. What, did she do ya, then *do* ya? Yer all alike, you men. A bird flips up 'er skirt an' ye'll do anything what she asks."

Evie moves quickly to leap onto Mrs. Powers again, teeth bared. But just as quickly, Charlie grips her around the waist, holding her back. Evie turns to look at him with murder in her own eyes.

"Let me kill 'er off, love," Evie begs him, "tha whole town'll be better off!"

"Two things, love," Charlie tells her, still holding on to her, "firstly, if we do, we're no better than the other vamps that get themselves killed, and we've got Brien and Bill, as well as the professor, and lots of others in town looking out for us. I don't think they'd be so keen if we just killed Mrs. Powers out of spite."

"They's vamps!?" whispers Watchman Masterson to Constable Waterstone, astonishingly, as if Mrs. Powers words were just now registering, "well *that* clears up a lot fer me. Did *you* know, constable?"

"Yes, mate, I knew," replies the constable, calmly "but not many others do, an' we don't want it gettin' out, you know how things get when there's some vamp claim. So-called 'slayers' an' all comin' ta a town, muckin' things up, gettin' folks all eggy, windin' 'em up. We don't want *that*, mate."

"Nah, s'pose not, constable," the watchman says, "still 'n' all, ain't they killas too?"

"Have you listened to anything what was said," asks the constable.

"And secondly," Charlie continues, "we already said that we'd only feed on blood that we got from our friends. Besides, she'll hang soon enough, then we can feed on *her* blood. Think of how satisfying that will be."

Evie calms down and her teeth recede with that and Charlie eases up on his vice-like grip.

"Constable," Evie asks, "Can we do that?"

"If she's dead, no laws on tha books says ya can't," he replies, "it'll also make tha body easier ta carry ta Potter's Field. So, have at it you two." And he grabs Mrs. Powers by the arm and leads her up the path to the carriage.

"Oh, no, ya can't," says Mrs. Powers, struggling against her restraints. "I ain't havin' my blood runnin' throo that body o' no vamp trallop 'n' 'er vamp lover."

"You ain't got nuffin ta say about it," the constable tells her as he leads her up to the side of the carriage, ready to put her in the back.

"But, but," Mrs. Powers stammers, "ya can't take me *blood*!"

"Where yer goin' ya ain't gonna need it, none," replies the watchman, "don't see why Evie 'n' Charlie can't have it, if'n it'll do 'em some good."

"Meanwhile, perfessor, Charlie, Evie, you go to tha stable in back an' just check tha horseshoe is tha right one."

"Of course, constable," the professor finally says. And the three head in back, they open the stable door and hear from the top of the path, "Get outta there, ya pillocks! 'At's *my* property. An' they're my 'orses."

"Shut yer gob," Watchman Masterson tells her. As they trio check on the horses, they hear the discussion continue at the top of the path:

They check the only horse in the barn and Evie brings out the horseshoe piece from her purse, and sure enough, the piece fits the broken horseshoe on the rear left hoof perfectly.

"Well," Charlie says, "guess that confirms it."

"Yes, I guess so," the constable agrees, and the three head back up the path to where Mrs Powers, Constable Waterstone and Watchman Masterson are awaiting the results.

"I've been a church-goer my whole life, an' my blood ain't goin' ta some unholy twat," Mrs. Powers tells them as they lift her into the back of the carriage.

"Yeah, a church-goin' killer, you are," says the constable. "Well, Charlie, Evie, we're goin' ta take 'er ta tha Nick. His honour, tha magistrate is due in town from Birmingham Wednesday next week, so it won't take us that long ta stretch 'er neck."

"So, constable," Evie calls to them, "tha piece we found fit 'er 'orse perfect. An' now she's defnitely gonna swing."

Mrs. Powers struggles against her restraints, but the large watchman climbs into the back of the carriage with her, and holds her down.

"You wait till my nephews get here, you lot," she screams at the men, "they'll make sure I'm treated fair. 'N' you, ya slag," she screams back at Evie, "you better hope they don't let me out or yer next!"

"I don't really think so," Evie says back just loud enough for Mrs. Powers to hear, "but if you wanna try that trap on me, c'mon, then, an' I'll give ya wot for, no matter what my Charlie says."

"'N' you say one more thing," the constable warns his prisoner, "'n' you can say g'bye ta a trial, we'll just hang ya here. An' I doubt that even yer nephews will muddy tha waters over it."

At that Mrs. Powers calms down and the constable, the watchman get ready to drive to the jail. The professor, who has just been taking it all in, climbs in the front of the carriage, next to the constable.

"Well, this certainly has been an eventful day, then, constable," he says, "I must give you all credit, I doubt that even the constabulary in London could have done a better bit of work. And you Charlie and Evie," he calls to them, "you were remarkable, and worry not, you two, there is no way anyone finds out anthing about you two from me, other than your help in this investigation."

"Thank you, perfessa," says the constable for them. "That relieves our minds here a great deal."

"Well, ya ain't gonna be so lucky with me," says Mrs. Powers from the rear.

"Oh, yes we are," the constable told her, "you are goin' ta be gagged durin' tha trial, so you can't say nuffin ta nobody,"

"*You* can't do tha'," Mrs Powers says defiantly.

"An' then, after tha trial for tha two or three days ya got left," the watchman added, "you'll be in the Nick, an' who's gonna believe you in there?" and he ties a dirty rag around her head, and into her mouth.

"Mmmm, mmmmph," she cries, but they fall on deaf ears as the constable gently claps the reigns signalling for the horse to move on.

"Well, love," Evie says, "guess we done good, yeah?"

"I think we've done really well, darlin'," Charlie tells her and grabs her around the waist, pulling her close and kissing her deeply. He reaches down and also grabs her fanny through her skirt. He manipulates it briefly and she grabs his hand.

"Well, look who wants ta get some now," she says laughingly, and kisses him right back just as deeply. She reaches down and grabs his organ through his trousers with her other other hand. "Well, love, I'd better take you home... now."

Chapter 25

BACK HOME

The trip home in the carriage was complete with kissing, fondling, prodding, and biting. It's a good thing Chauncy knew the way back the five houses to Mr. Firthe's stable. It's just turned sunset by the time they arrive back home. They just finish putting Chauncy into his stall and the carriage outside the stable. Charlie is about to put the bridles away, when Evie grabs his attention.

"What ya think?" she asks him. He looks over at the sound of her voice. He sees that she has tossed aside her hood and tied herself up to the stable wall with a bridle hung on one of the posts. Her hands are over her head and her feet are barely touching the ground. Her breasts are heaving in anticipation. Her eyes are glazed over with passion.

"C'mon lover," Evie sing-songs, "I promise I'll resist ya. *That* should be fun."

Charlie grabs her top and yanks the material in half. Her breath is coming even faster now.

"No, no, ya vamp," she shouts. "I ain't gonna let ya fuck *me*!" And she clamps her legs together.

He yanks down her skirt and he smells her fanny is dripping and pungent. He forces her thighs apart and puts his hands on her body, manipulating her clit with one and probing her vagina with three fingers of the other. Evie is wriggling and moving whilst still "tied up" in the bridles. She pretends to to resist, but her passion is getting the best of her as her legs come further apart. He grabs Evie by her thighs and digs his face in her mound. He licks her clit and inserts his tongue into her body as she squirms in ecstacy. He keeps up his oral stimulations until she orgasms between his lips. It's only the first one of the evening and there will be many more to come before they collapse, probably close to dawn when they have to rest at any rate. Of course with their new hoods, that situation has become much more manageable.

He reaches up and loosens her hands from the bridle and carries her naked body silently into the house, it's lucky that Mr. Firthe is nowhere to be seen. Not that they's need to explain how it was that she was being carried nude from the barn to the house. But better not have to answer those questions. They reach the house and Evie opens the door whilst in Charlie's arms. As soon as they are inside, she adjusts her body position so that her legs are over her shoulders, her fanny directly in front of his face and she reaches up and digs her nails into the ceiling of the front room and crosses her feet around his head, drawing his face into her fanny again. Charlie grabs her arse, pulling her even more deeply into his mouth again. He can smell the previous orgasm still on her as he licks, sucks, nibbles and probes the inner reaches of her womanhood. She squirms and screams wildly as she orgasms again.

Then she dislodges herself from his and her grasps, and dashes into the bedroom. Charlie takes his cloak and clothing off as he leaves a trail going into the bedroom to see her laying spread out arms and legs splayed out on the bed. His own organ is erect and there's liquid slipping out of he tip. He mounts her and easily slips himself into her still-dewy vagina. As soon as he is inside her completely, she rolls over so that now she is on top and pounds away at him, rasing and lowering herself on his organ. After a time of their mutual growling, and snarling, he grabs her shoulders, throwing her onto her back on the bed, erect penis still inside her. They scratch, gouge and bite each other to satiate their love for each other. He explodes inside her as she screams with her own satisfaction.

"So, love," Charlie says, breathlessly "you call that resisting?"

The Nottingham Journal has lurid accounts of the murders, Mrs. Powers' arrest and her execution in the town square. However, nowhere is there even a mention of Charlie and Evie's participation in the investigation or of the fact that they are members of he undead community. All accounts of the events have been given them by Constable Waterstone and Professor McWilliams, according to the articles.

Evie and Charlie stay in his house for the rest of that decade and several others. There are small crimes during that time, of course, but nothing so serious that Constable Waterstone needs their assistance on. They continue to survive on the nourishment that The Flying Horse and The White Star can supply them. No one comes looking for creatures of the night and for a long time, they are content wo walk about, feed and fuck with impunity. They don't need any money as with Mrs. Powers no longer in the picture, the rent Charlie had been paying is now a moot point. And her nephews have no interest in maintaining the upkeep of the properties or on having to collect rent each and every month.

However, after 60 years of bliss, Charlie and Evie's special skills are needed once again, as a new threat and new killings are threatening the placid life in a new Nottingham.

The End

CPSIA information can be obtained
at www.ICGtesting.com
Printed in the USA
BVHW050224081222
653755BV00005B/125